"You yanked the rug out from under me, Jewel, and I didn't take it well."

"I—I know. And I'm sorry—"

"Not your problem. And I mean that."

"Oh." She bit off another chunk of her burger, although her insides were shaking so much—and not only from the cold, despite the fire—she doubted she could get it down.

"So," Silas said, sitting again. "You find someplace to stay yet?"

He *would* bring that up. "'Fraid not."

"When you're ready to move in, then, let me know."

Jewel stared at his profile for what seemed like forever before saying, very quietly, "You sure?"

"Not a bit."

She understood completely.

Dear Reader,

"I guess I'm ready now."

That's how, more than thirty years ago, my husband proposed to me. Because, y'know, "Will you marry me?" would have been *such* a cliché. Of course, *I'd* been ready practically from the moment we met more than five years before, when I was (gulp!) twenty…but, bless him, he knew I needed more time to ripen before taking that big step. Considering the challenges that came with raising the five sons who showed up over the next fifteen years…he was right!

Although sometimes, as Jewel Jasper and Silas Garrett (Eli's brother from *A Marriage-Minded Man*) discover in *Adding Up to Marriage,* not being "ready" is another way of saying "I'm scared…of being hurt, of being abandoned, of making a mistake. Of not being who I need you to be." Especially in Jewel's case, whose life hasn't exactly given her a lot of examples of how to keep a relationship going. Girlfriend's convinced she'll *never* be "ready"…until Silas rocks her preconceived notions all to heck and makes her reassess a thing or three.

Because the right person will do that.

Enjoy.

Karen Templeton

ADDING UP TO MARRIAGE

KAREN TEMPLETON

Silhouette

SPECIAL EDITION®

Published by Silhouette Books

America's Publisher of Contemporary Romance

SILHOUETTE BOOKS

ISBN-13: 978-0-373-65555-7

Recycling programs
for this product may
not exist in your area.

ADDING UP TO MARRIAGE

Visit Silhouette Books at www.eHarlequin.com

Printed in U.S.A.

Books by Karen Templeton

KAREN TEMPLETON

Since 1998, RITA® Award winner and Waldenbooks best-seller Karen Templeton has written more than thirty books for the Harlequin and Silhouette lines. A transplanted Easterner, she now lives in New Mexico with two hideously spoiled cats and whichever of her five sons happens to be in residence.

Acknowledgments

To Jules Johnstun
CPM, LM, LDEM, PES
who enthusiastically answered my questions
about being a home-birth midwife
in northern New Mexico.
The plastic pelvis? Totally her idea.

Dedication

To Vista Care Hospice in Albuquerque
without whose above-and-beyond support
during the most stressful months of my life
this book would not have happened.

To Mama
1912–2010
Here's hoping there's ham, chocolate and dogs
in Heaven!

And
to my beloved husband Jack
1942–2010
whose above-and-beyond support
for everything I did
and everything I was
is sorely missed.
Love you.

Chapter One

Seated behind the computer in the woodworking shop's cramped, cluttered office, Silas Garrett caught the blur of color zip past the open door. Then back. Then finally light in the doorway.

"Oh! Hi!" a breathless, bubbly Jewel Jasper called over the whine of saws ripping lumber, a booming *"...mañana en Santa Fe y Taos..."* from the Spanish talk radio station. "Noah around?"

Silas couldn't help it—every time he saw her the image of a cute little bunny popped into his head. And not, alas, the sort clad in skimpy satin, bow ties and high heels.

Even more unfortunately, if Jewel—with her shiny brown ponytail and her big, blue-gray eyes behind her delicate oval glasses and her skimpy, ruffly sweater buttoned over her even skimpier breasts—was a bunny, his brother, Noah, was definitely the Big Bad Wolf. Fine, so Silas was mixing his fairy tales, but he doubted it was much of a stretch to suppose the Big Bad Wolf occasionally dined on bunny.

Especially if the bunny kept hopping across the wolf's path.

This had to make the third or fourth time in as many weeks the midwife-in-training, temporarily living in the house another Garrett brother had vacated after his marriage, had popped in—or hopped in, in this case—on the pretext of "needing" Noah to fix something or other in the quasi-adobe.

"Sorry." Jabbing his own glasses back into place, Silas returned his gaze to the bookkeeping program on the screen. Numbers, he got. Women, not so much. Especially women who fell for his brother's chicanery. "Not here. Won't be until later." He entered a figure, then forced himself to be polite, despite all that ingenuousness taking a toll on his good humor. "Care to leave a message?"

"It's the roof again," Jewel said, inviting herself in and plunking her baggy-pantsed bottom on the cracked plastic chair across from Silas. Why, God only knew. "Over the living room, this time. I'm really sorry to be such a pain—especially since I'm not even paying rent!—but I can't exactly get up there and fix it myself."

She giggled. Silas's least favorite sound in the world. From anyone over ten, at least. Then her pale little forehead bunched.

"If Eli's fixing to sell it, I don't imagine he wants to keep repairing water damage. Oh—and I tried to make a fire the other night and ohmigosh, there was smoke everywhere!" Her hands fluttered. Visual aids. "So I'm guessing the chimney's blocked—oh! Noah!" She bounced up when his younger, bigger, buffer brother appeared. Damn. "Silas said you wouldn't be back until later!"

Slapping his denim jacket on a rack by the door, Noah

barely spared Jewel a glance before tossing a crumpled stack of receipts on the desk. "From the Manning project," he said, swiping his muscled forearm across his sweaty forehead. "Figured I'd better get 'em to you before I lost track—"

"Noah?" Jewel tapped his shoulder. "Sorry to bug you, but the roof needs attention. Again. And the chimney's clogged, too."

Noah shot Silas the same "why me?" look he did every time Jewel made an appearance. Since even wolves, apparently, could be picky. And Jewel was not, apparently, on Noah's menu. Although for how long, Silas surmised, was anybody's guess. Since not having a hankering for myopic bunnies this week didn't mean he wouldn't at some point.

However, it still being this week, Noah cut his eyes to Jewel, nodded, mumbled, "I'll send someone over," and walked away.

Jewel collapsed in a deflated heap on the chair again, clutching the seat edges on either side of nonexistent hips. "Honestly. You'd think I had cooties or something."

Wondering *Why are you still here?* Silas muttered, "Did it ever occur to you he's not interested?"

She straightened, her rosy little mouth pursed. "There is that, I suppose. But…" Standing, she yanked down the hem of the short sweater. Despite at least two other layers—a T-shirt and a tank top, neither of which matched the sweater or each other—it was quite evident, in the early fall chill permeating the small room, that she wasn't wearing a bra. "I thought Noah was more equal opportunity than that. And did you know you're staring at my boobs?"

Silas jerked his gaze back to the screen. "Sorry."

"No, actually it's kinda flattering, since most men don't take notice."

Oh, for cripes' sake...

Giving up, Silas leaned back in his father's chair, his hands laced over his stomach. In a small town like Tierra Rosa you knew everybody, by reputation at least if not personally. So between what he'd heard and what he'd seen, he'd concluded Jewel was the strangest mixture of naive and world-weary he'd ever met. And God knows he'd met his fair share of women. Even if not solely by choice, his mother having sworn to end his single-father days if it killed her. In fact, how Jewel had thus far slipped Donna Garrett's radar was a mystery.

Especially as Silas had no doubt his mother would think Jewel was perfect for him. Being female and breathing and all.

"I don't get it—why are you so determined to hook up with my brother?"

"And what earthly difference does it make to you? Or do you discuss Noah with all his girlfriends?"

Whoa. Bunny had a bite. Who knew?

"First, to call them 'girlfriends' might be pushing it," Silas said, having no idea how to answer the first part of her question. "Second...no. Hell, half the time I have no idea who he's...seeing."

Arms folded over the nipples. "They why single me out?"

He didn't figure she'd appreciate the bunny analogy. "Because I seriously doubt you know what you're getting into. Noah isn't, uh, exactly looking for forever."

Her gaze sharpened. *"First,"* she said, mimicking him, "you're a lot safer staring at my breasts than patronizing me. Second, I'm well aware of your brother's reputation—"

"But you just know you're the one who can make him change, right?"

"Change?" She burst out laughing. "Boy, have you got

the wrong end of the stick. I'm no more interested in settling down right now than I am in growing horns. Which is why Noah would be perfect. All I'm looking for is…a little fun. Somebody who isn't interested in 'serious' any more than I am." Now her eyes narrowed. "So if you could, you know, kinda drop that hint…?"

After several seconds' of Silas's silent glare, she shrugged, then stood, sighing out, "It was worth a shot," before hiking to the door…only to swivel back in her black-and-white checked rubber-soled flats. With red daisies over the toes. "But you really need to lighten up, Silas. You are *way* too tense."

Then she was gone, leaving Silas staring blankly at the computer screen, his shoulders knotted.

"She gone?" he heard a minute later.

"Not nearly far enough, I don't imagine."

Palming his short brown hair, Noah exhaled. Loudly. "She's a sweet kid and all, but…not my type."

"Seriously?"

"Dude. She's like, twelve."

"Actually, she's somewhere in her mid-twenties. Well past legal but nowhere near desperate. Your perfect woman, in other words," he said, through inexplicably gritted teeth.

Noah seemed to consider this for a moment, then shook his head, and Silas's teeth unclenched. "Nah. Cute hasn't been my thing for a couple of years now."

"Then perhaps you should tell her that. Although maybe not in those exact words."

"I *have*. Several times. All she does is get this goofy—and yet, eerily knowing—look on her face." He paused. "Not that she doesn't have a certain weird appeal—"

"Hence the eerily knowing look."

Another moment of consideration, another head shake.

"Nope, not caving. Not this time. Shoot, it would be like taking candy from a baby. Besides—" his younger brother grinned "—I met this gal in Española last weekend…"

"Don't want to know," Silas said as the phone rang. Chuckling, Noah waved and was gone before Silas answered. "Garrett Woodworks—"

"The boys are fine," his mother said, well aware of Silas's tendency to freak whenever she called while watching his two young sons. "Me, however…" She sighed. "I was bringing in some firewood and *somebody* left a toy truck on the porch step, and I tripped over it and fell—would've made a great America's Funniest Home Video—and now my ankle's all big and purple. Ollie says it looks like Barney—"

Phone still in hand, Silas hit three wrong keys before finally logging out of the program, then rocketed from the chair. "On my way—"

"Why don't you see if Jewel's around, let her have a look at it?"

So much for the not-on-his-mother's-radar theory. "She delivers babies, Mom. I'm guessing you're done with all that."

"She's also a nurse, smarty pants."

True. Unfortunately. "Fine. If she's home, I'll bring her."

"Good. Oh, and—" Donna lowered her voice "—you might want to hurry before the boys realize they could set the house on fire and there wouldn't be a darn thing I could do about it."

Plugged into her MP3 player, Jewel flinched when she opened her door to find Silas punching his arms into his corduroy jacket sleeves and looking extremely annoyed. But then—as he indicated she needed to ditch the earbuds—when was he ever not?

"My mother messed up her ankle. She asked if you wouldn't mind coming over."

Yep, caught that emphasis, all righty. Then his words sank in. "Ohmigosh—" she shoved her bare feet back into her shoes, yanked her sweatercoat off the hook by the door and pushed past him and down the stairs "—does she think it's broken?"

"No idea." She heard the door shut, Silas catch up with her. "But she said it was real swollen. And purple."

"Might only be a sprain," Jewel said, tucking her chin into her chest against the suddenly frigid breeze—September in northern New Mexico tended to be fickle—as she hotfooted it down the flagstone walk. At the end she made a sharp left, only to practically get whiplash when Silas grabbed her elbow and lugged her toward his Explorer, parked in front of the house.

"Quicker this way," he said, hauling open her door, then zipping around the hood, the wind wreaking havoc on his normally neat, dark brown hair and probably irritating the very life out of him. Oh, yeah, Jewel had him pegged, all right—a man who prefers his universe precise and orderly, thank you very much, and woe betide anything or anybody who disturbs it. Or him.

Silas climbed in, rammed his key into the ignition. Glanced over, all Heathcliffian glower. "Seat belt."

"For heaven's sake, it's two blocks—"

"Seat. Belt. Now."

Sighing, Jewel secured the lap belt, only to release it less than thirty seconds later. Without, it should be noted, passing a single other vehicle. But considering the don't-mess slant to Silas's mouth, she opted to let it go.

The moment they were out of the car, the Garretts' white

front door swung open to expel a pair of wide-eyed, agitated little boys. The younger one, a curly blond cherub of maybe four or so, made a beeline for his father and grabbed his hand.

"Gramma fell and hurt her foot!" he said, tugging him inside. "It's *huge!* I gave her the phone so she could call you!"

"Did not!" the older boy said, his straight, wheat-colored bangs blowing every which way in the breeze as he smacked his younger brother's shoulder.

"Did too—"

"Boys. Not now," Silas said with the sort of quiet authority that makes a person go, *Whoa.* The little one now clinging to him like a koala, he shut the door and crossed to his mother, seated on the old blue sofa with her foot propped up, her graying red hair a distressed tangle around her very pale face. Jewel took one look and shook her head.

"Silas, go put a whole bunch of ice in a plastic bag and wrap it in a towel, bring it here. But no sense in me even examining it. The ice might take down the swelling some, but if that's not a candidate for the x-ray machine, I don't know what is."

Donna simultaneously winced and sighed. "I don't suppose it helps that I heard a cracking sound when I went down."

"Not a good sign, no. Still…" Jewel carefully sat by the offending foot, nodding her thanks to Silas when he returned with the ice pack. "It might not be that bad," she said, carefully cushioning Donna's ankle in the ice pack before looking up at Silas, "but you should probably get her to the ER."

"Yes, of course, absolutely. Okay, boys, go get in the car—"

"For goodness' sake, Si," Donna said. "They can't go

with us! Who knows how long it'll take? Besides, an ER waiting room's no place for children."

"Like they're both not on first-name basis with the staff already," Silas said. Donna gave him a look. "Fine. But who's gonna watch 'em? Noah's clear across town at the Mannings, Eli and Dad are in Santa Fe. We could drop them off at Jess's, but that's a good half hour out of our way—"

"Um, hello?" Jewel raised her hand. "I'd be happy to keep an eye on them." She aimed a smile in the boys' direction, only to be met with a pair of dubious frowns.

"See?" Donna said, her face contorting as she shifted her ample form to put her good foot on the floor. "The Good Lord provides."

Silas's gaze shot to Jewel's. "I'm not sure that's such a good idea—"

"Nonsense. Oliver?" This in a strained voice to the straight-haired one. "Get my poncho from the closet, honey. And Tad, grab my purse off the table by the door. That's right, sugars—bring 'em to me—"

"I don't want to stay with her!" The little one inched closer to Silas, his worried eyes nearly the same muddy green as his father's. "What if she's mean?"

Jewel gasped. "I'm not—"

"Oh, for heaven's sake," Donna said as Oliver dumped the well-worn, Peruvian-patterned poncho on the couch beside her, "Jewel helps deliver babies! She obviously *loves* children! Don't you, honey?"

"You bet! And really, Silas, it's no problem. I don't have any appointments today or anything." Although despite the generous amount of cheer she'd injected into the words— what with her lack of pressing obligation being momentarily convenient—overall this was not a good thing. As

in, she had far too much free time on her hands and not
nearly enough cash in them—

"So it's settled," Donna said. "You all can stay right here.
Si, give me a hand—"

"But we can't stay here!" Oliver put in, his dark brown
eyes all watery. "It's almost time to feed Doughboy!"

Oh, for pity's sake...

Crouching in front of the child, Jewel smiled. "Tell you
what—if it's okay with your daddy, we can go to your
house, and you can feed Doughboy—" who or whatever
that was "—and if it gets late you can go right to sleep in
your own beds. But before that," she then said to Tad, tapping him on his nose, "we're gonna have so much fun your
daddy's gonna be sorry he wasn't with us!"

The boys shared a glance...then a shrug. Jewel couldn't
decide if that was good or not. Then her mouth fell open
as Silas scooped his mother—who was by no means a frail
little thing—into his arms, before, with no outward evidence of strain, carting her across the room and out the
still open front door.

"My daddy's strong, huh?" little curly-head said, grinning at Jewel with one of those sweet, baby-toothed grins
designed to make a woman want to rush right out and fill
her womb.

Especially when said womb had just been nicely primed
by the sight of a good-looking man acting all manly and
such. Silently cursing biological imperatives and what-not,
Jewel took her little charges by the hand, deciding it was
best all around if she not answer that question.

"You know," Silas said to his mother many hours later
on their way home from the hospital, "you seem awfully
mellow for somebody with a broken ankle."

Beside him, Donna released a half laugh. "That's the

pain meds." She looked down at her foot, splinted to within an inch of its life. "Might be tricky to cook with this thing on. Your father will be beside himself."

"I imagine he'll live. Besides, that's what the church ladies are for. After the thousands of casseroles you've made for everybody else over the years, they owe you."

She laughed again, then sighed. "Shame I won't be able to take care of the boys, though—"

"And don't even think about that. Hey, if I have to, I'll keep 'em with me. It could work," he said to his mother's hoot of laughter.

"These are Ollie and Tad we're talking about. Otherwise known as Thing One and Thing Two?"

"Thought you said they'd calmed down."

"I lied."

He glanced at his mother. "And you didn't think to warn Jewel?"

"Gal has youth on her side. And resilience. She'll be fine. But wasn't it providential, how she was available to babysit? She's a real sweetheart, that one. A *real* sweetheart."

Oh, hell. "You know, you could at least *try* to be subtle. Next I'm gonna find out you deliberately broke your ankle just to further your matchmaking mission—hey. Everything okay?"

Donna nodded tightly. "Joy juice is wearing off, I suspect."

"So take more."

"Forget it. A flower child I may have been, but a druggie? Never. Damned if I'm about to start now. I'll be fine," she said, her chin lifting. "At least until we get home."

Silas's eyes again slid to his mother, the stress lines bracketing her mouth attesting to her no longer being the bottomless well of energy she'd once been. "Why didn't you say something before? About the kids, I mean."

A moment ticked by before she quietly said, "Because after what happened...those babies needed mothering. And since I was the only candidate... Oh, don't get that look on your face, I'm only stating the facts. At least I was there to fill the gap."

"Since I haven't done anything to fill it myself."

She shrugged. Woman could say more with a shrug than most women say in a thirty-minute conversation. Then she blew out a long breath.

"I adore those little monkeys, you know that. But even before this happened, I'd begun to realize I'm not as up to chasing them as I'd thought. As I want to be. Occasionally is fine—well, once this blasted ankle is better—but full time?" She shook her head. "I'm so tired by the time evening rolls around I can barely have a conversation with your father." That was followed by a weary chuckle. "Let alone anything else."

"Mom, geez."

His mother laughed again, then briefly squeezed his arm. "I'm sorry, Silas. The spirit's willing, but—"

"And there's nothing to be sorry for." He flashed a smile at her, even as panic began to simmer in his gut. Nobody knew better than he that both his sons had gotten double doses of snips and snails and puppy dog tails. Not to mention enough energy to fuel a hydrogen bomb. Finding another day-care option for them wasn't going to be easy. But taking out his mother—who'd already earned her medal for surviving her own four boys—hadn't been part of the game plan. "You could've backed out anytime, you know."

In the dim light from the dash, he saw tears glisten in his mother's warm brown eyes. "Couldn't. Would've meant giving them up."

"It's okay, we'll figure something out," he said softly as they pulled into his parents' driveway, his father shooting through the front door before Silas switched off the engine.

Nearly thirty-four years his parents had been married, and yet Gene Garrett's solicitous concern for his wife when he jerked open her door was every bit as tender as Silas remembered from his childhood. Oh, they fussed at each other as much as the next couple, but what they had—it was magic and rare and defied explanation. Or definition.

And there were times when Silas envied them so much it hurt.

"For heaven's sake, Gene," Donna said after Silas's dad gingerly maneuvered her out of the truck. No mean feat. "I'm completely capable of managing on my own. Thank you, honey," she said to Silas after he handed her the crutches. She squinted at the things for a moment, shaking her head, then fitted them under her arms, her grip firm on the braces. "But you better go on—I imagine Jewel's more than ready to be rescued by now."

"It's nearly ten—the boys are bound to be asleep." His mother rolled her eyes, and he smiled. "You sure you don't need me?"

"Honestly, between you and Gene... It's a broken ankle, for goodness' sake, not bubonic plague! Here, hold this," she said to Gene, shoving a crutch at him, then reached up to give Silas a strong, one-armed hug around his neck. "Thanks for everything, honey. And we'll talk tomorrow."

Still, after Silas climbed back into the truck to watch his father hover over his mother as she unsteadily navigated the short sidewalk between the driveway and house, envy pinched again. And regret, that his own marriage had been a dismal failure.

But at twenty-four, even with his parents' example, he hadn't been nearly as ready for it as he'd thought. Especially to a gal who'd apparently tuned out when the minister, during their prenuptial classes, had done his best to drive home that married life wasn't all sunshine and rainbows, that it took more than love—and sex—to get through the rough patches. That without determination to *make* it work, a willingness to put each other's feelings and needs ahead of your own from time to time, you didn't have a chance in hell.

Not that he had used those exact words, but close enough.

And God knew Silas had tried his best. He'd hated see-ing Amy so miserable, especially after Bundle of Joy Two arrived. But as her demands became increasingly impos-sible to meet—she constantly complained about not having enough money, yet pitched a fit if he worked late because he wasn't around to help her with the babies—Silas began to see the writing on the wall.

Oh, he'd dug in his heels the first time she'd said she wanted out, not about to give up that easily on something he still believed in. But eventually Silas had had to admit he couldn't prop up the marriage on his own. Or raise his wife as well as his sons.

His folks inside, Silas backed out of the drive, thinking that at least the resulting implosion, as horrendous as it had been, hadn't left him where it had found him. In fact, his shrugging off his mother's relentless matchmaking attempts notwithstanding, he was beginning to heal, even if only in terms of…*maybe. If* the right woman—not girl, *woman*— crossed his path, he might, *might,* consider trying again.

But this time, he had a checklist as long as his arm, with *Putting the boys first* at the top. Followed closely by maturity. Serenity. Stability.

Sanity.

In other words, not someone who made him feel like the ground was constantly shifting under his feet.

Moments later he pulled up into his driveway and cut the engine, his forehead crunched. Why were the lights still on?

The cottonwood's first crackly, fallen leaves scampered across his feet as he walked to the door, the rustle barely audible over the raucous goings-on inside. The instant he opened the heavy carved door to the hundred-year-old adobe, Doughboy speed-waddled over and plastered himself against Silas's calf, the English bulldog's underbite trembling underneath bulging, terror-stricken eyes.

Why? Why you send crazy lady here?

Then, his spawn's shrieks of unbridled glee assaulting his ears, Silas got the first glimpse of what had once been his living room.

Which now looked like Tokyo, post-Godzilla-rampage.

Chapter Two

"**D**addy! *Daddy!* You're home—!"

"You shoulda been here, we had sooooo much fun!"

"So I see," Silas said in a low, controlled voice as he swept Tad up onto his hip while leveling a *What the hell?* look past the destruction at the flushed, heavily breathing, messy-haired female responsible for the mayhem.

Who gave him a whatchagonnado? shrug.

Woman destroys his house and she gives him a *shrug?* God help him.

And her.

Sofa and chair cushions teetered in unstable towers all over the room. Sheets, tablecloths, bedspreads—was that his good *comforter?*—shrouded every flat surface. No lamp was where he'd left it that morning, not a single picture on the wall was straight. And so many toys littered the floor— what he could see of it—it looked like Santa's sleigh had upchucked.

Leaning against his ankle, the dog moaned. *See? Told ya.*

Jewel giggled. "Guess we kinda got carried away."

Silas forced himself to breathe. "Ya think?"

Apparently, she got the message. "O-kay, guys, Daddy's home, so off to bed—no, no arguments, we had a deal, remember?"

He could only imagine. "Thought I said bedtime was eight?"

"You did, but—"

"Jewel said if we took our baths and got our jammies on," Ollie said, "we could stay up for a bit."

"A bit?" Silas said. Calmly. Over the seething rage. "It's after ten."

"What? You're kidding!" Shoving loose pieces of hair behind her ears, Jewel picked her way through the wreckage to peer at the cable box clock. "Ohmigosh—I'm so sorry! The clock got covered and we were having so much fun we lost track of time—"

"Yeah," Tad said, curls bobbing. "We made cookies, an' then Jewel said we could bring our toys out here, an' then we decided to make tunnels an' stuff—"

"Jewel's like the funnest person ever," Ollie put in. "She's not like a grownup at all!"

There's an understatement, Silas thought as he lowered the four-year-old to his feet, then lightly swatted both pajama-covered bottoms. "Go get your teeth brushed, I'll be there in a sec—"

"But we already brushed our teeth!" Ollie said, then stretched his lips back to show. "Shee?"

"Fine. Let's go, then. And you," he said, pointing at Jewel, "stay right where you are."

She shrugged again, then plucked the boys' quilts off two chairs. "Here! Take these back to your room!" The kids ran over, grabbed the quilts, gave Jewel hugs and kisses, and took off down the hall. Where, naturally, somebody tripped over his quilt, taking his brother down in the process, resulting in a tangle of Thomas the Tank Engines and hysterically giggling little boys. Silas sighed, sorted out his spawn and steered them to their room as Doughboy trudged dutifully behind, leaving a trail of slobber in his wake.

The boys flew into their beds on opposite sides of the room hard enough to bang both headboards into the walls, while poor Doughboy collapsed on the multicolored carpet in the center of the floor with a noisy, relieved sigh. His little masters, however, were still high as kites from overexertion and God only knew how much sugar. In fact, no sooner had Silas tucked Tad's quilt around him than he yanked back the covers, yelled "Gotta pee!" and flew to the bathroom, leaping over the already snoring dog.

Silas looked at his older son. "What about you?"

"No, I'm good," Ollie said, pawing through two dozen stuffed animals for his ratty, shredded baby blanket which at this rate would accompany the kid to college. His bankie found, the kid pushed out a satisfied sigh and wriggled into the middle of the critters, giggling when Silas momentarily buried him in the comforter. Then his head popped out, his straight hair all staticky and his expression suddenly serious.

"Is Gramma okay?"

Silas sat on the bed beside him, rearranging the covers. "She'll be fine, but her ankle really is broken. Which means she's not gonna be able to take care of you guys."

Worry instantly flooded big, brown eyes. "So who's gonna watch us?"

"I have no idea. That's tomorrow's project. In the meantime, you get to hang out with me. Guess I'll have to work from home for a while."

"We tried that before, remember? You nearly lost it."

As tired as he was, Silas laughed. "That was a year ago. You're older now. It'll be fine."

The toilet flushed; Tad zoomed back into the room and flew into his bed again. Unlike his brother, Tad didn't need to sleep with a menagerie. But God help them all if Moothy—a smelly, one-eyed moose with sagging antlers—went AWOL.

"Okay, you two," Silas said, bending over to kiss Tad. "Lights out—"

"Book?" Tad flopped around to grab a Dr. Seuss from the skyscraper-high pile on the floor beside the bed.

"Not tonight, buddy. I'd pass out if I tried to read right now."

"Besides, doofus," Ollie said, "Jewel read like ten books to us already, remember?"

Curling himself around Moothy, Tad sulked. "S'not the same if Daddy doesn't do it."

Just reach in there and squeeze my heart, why not? "I'm flattered, squirt, but reading is not happening tonight. So lights out. Now."

Grumbling, Tad reached over to turn off his light. Much to Silas's relief, the kid nearly passed out before Silas finished with the nightly hugs and kisses routine, but Ollie still had enough oomph to whisper, "You know what?"

"What?"

"I think Jewel should be our babysitter."

"She's already got a job," Silas said as he smoothed back his son's soft, straight hair. "She was just filling in because it was an emergency." *And I would hang myself if she was the only option.* "But…I'm glad you had fun with her."

"Are you kidding? She's like the coolest girl ever!"

Yeah, let's hear it for the cool girls, Silas thought, returning to the living room. Like a hummingbird, Jewel madly darted from spot to spot, folding, straightening, picking up. At Silas's entrance, she glanced over only to disappear behind a tablecloth as she stretched her arms to fold it in half.

"Nothing's broken," she said from behind the cloth, then reappeared, the cloth neatly folded into eighths in three swift, graceful moves. "In case you were wondering."

Glued to the spot, Silas watched her zip, zap, zing around the room as he got grumpier by the second. "But where do you get off going into *my* room and getting *my* comforter off of *my* bed?" Silas said. Okay, whined. "I sleep under that! Naked! And now it's dirty!"

In the midst of hauling a cushion larger than she was back onto the sofa, Jewel shot him a look. "Geez, it might be a little dusty in places, but it's not *dirty.* And the boys brought it out, I didn't go into your room and disturb your things. Trust me, I'm not that desperate."

For what? floated through Silas's brain, only to get shoved aside by Jewel's "You sleep naked?" as she scooted across the room to smack at several large smudges on the comforter.

It took a second. "I sleep *what?*"

That got another look. A puzzled one, this time. "Naked. You know, without any clothes?"

"I know what it means! But isn't that kind of a personal question?"

She frowned at him. "Um…okay…it wasn't me who introduced the word into the conversation. You did."

"I did not!"

"Yes, you did," she said patiently. "Because my imagination's not that vivid. Not that it matters to me one way or the other." Huffing a little, she dragged the king-size comforter off the dining table, only to have it swallow her whole as she tried to fold it, like she was wrestling a monster marshmallow. Finally she gave up and dumped it on the sofa. "But you don't strike me as the sleeping-naked type."

"Could we please move on?"

"You're really cute when you blush. And it's okay, really. Since I do, too."

"Do what?"

"Sleep naked. You hungry?"

Lord above, being in the same room with her was like riding the Tilt-A-Whirl at the fair. Over the dizziness, Silas watched her zip to the kitchen, ignoring—more or less—the way her butt twitched as she walked. Then he opened his mouth to say "no," that all he wanted was for this night to be over, but then he realized, one, that his stomach felt like it was going to eat itself and, two, that the house smelled like an Italian restaurant.

Against his better judgment, he let his gaze sweep what he could see of his kitchen from where he stood. As he feared, it made Armageddon look like a minor dustup. The sooner he got this chick out of his house, the better. Except—

"Damn. I should've run you home before I put the boys to bed."

"Oh! That's okay, I figured you'd get back late. So I called Patrice, asked her to come get me in a little while. We've got a couple clients to see early tomorrow out at Jemez, so I'll probably crash at her house, since it's halfway to the pueblo already."

The idea of this woman being responsible for bringing someone's baby into the world made him shudder. But then, childbirth was a messy business, too, so he supposed she felt right at home. He looked at his kitchen again.

"There's actual food in there somewhere?"

"Just something I tossed together out of whatever you had on hand," she said, shoving aside...stuff to plunk a casserole dish onto the counter. "Go on, you sit—" she pointed at the formal dining table behind him "—I'll warm some of this up and bring it right over. I see you've got beer—you want one?"

He sat, becoming one with the chair. "Please."

A minute later she set a heaping dish of her concoction in front of him—pasta and tomato sauce and sausage and peppers and cheese and heaven knew what else. *And you'll eat it and love it,* he thought, almost too hungry to care.

"Huh," he said, taking a second bite over the clatter of pans, water rushing into the sink. "This is really good."

"Thanks. Tell me if you want more, there's plenty. You eat while I clean."

But once he'd taken the edge off his hunger, he felt weird sitting here while she was in there cleaning. So he got up and moved his plate and beer to the breakfast bar, climbing up on the stool.

"Aw...didja get lonely?" she said with a little smile as she wiped down the island. A throwaway question, hardly meant to cause the pang it did. When he didn't answer she tossed him another glance, then sashayed to the sink to rinse out the sponge. "So how's your mom?"

"Looks like she'll be out of commission for a while," Silas said around another mouthful of food. "She's in a splint until the swelling goes down enough to put on a cast. It'll definitely put a cramp in her style, that's for sure. And mine. I'll have to make other day-care arrangements."

"Well..." Jewel's entire face scrunched in thought. "I've heard lots of good things about the Baptist preschool. And there's that place out on the highway, in the old convenience store Thea Griego used to live in?"

"With the big jungle mural across the front?"

"Yep. I know the gal who runs it, she's the real deal. Although they might be full up at the moment—"

"It's okay," Silas said, almost irritably. "I'll check around in the morning. So...what all went on in here while I was gone?"

Jewel laughed. "What *didn't* go on, is more like it. And I apologize for keeping them up so late, but they were having so much fun—well, me, too, but that's something else again—I didn't have the heart to play mean old babysitter and make them go to bed. Especially since I doubted they would've gone to sleep on time, anyway. They missed you," she said with a little smile. "And they were so worried about their grandma. And no way was I gonna let them sit in front of the TV all night, no, sir."

Dinner dishes scraped and rinsed, she pushed down the dishwasher door and pulled out the bottom rack. "So we made cookies—they're on that dish over there if you want some—" she nodded toward a foil-covered plate at the end of the bar "—and read a bunch of books—I made Ollie read a couple to me, he sounds like he could use the practice—and then we played about a million games of Snakes and Ladders, and then we played Secret City."

"Which called for wholesale destruction of my living room."

She straightened, shoving a piece of hair off her forehead with her wrist. Even with her glasses, he could see the knot between her brows. "Kids learn by playing, Silas. By using their imaginations. Okay, so maybe we sorta went overboard—I'm sorry about your living room. But I put it all back together, didn't I? And the boys had *fun*. Isn't that kinda the whole point of being a kid?"

Life's not all about having fun, he wanted to say, except even he knew how stuffy and ridiculous it would have sounded. And of course he wanted the kids to have fun, but...

But, what? Yeah, that's right—no answer, huh?

His dinner finished, Silas reached for the foil-covered plate. Catching a whiff of the peanut butter cookies lurking underneath, he smiled. Despite himself.

"You might want to put peanut butter on your list," Jewel said, her back to him as she continued cleaning. "I got carried away with that, too."

Silas bit into one, sighing at the taste of childhood, of innocence against his tongue, and felt like a heel. "Where'd you get the flour?"

"One of your neighbors. Which reminds me, you owe Mrs. Maple two cups of flour. And an egg."

Silas hesitated, hoping she'd turn around. She didn't. "These are delicious, too."

She shrugged. Silas sighed.

"Jewel, it's been a long day and I'm ready to drop, but that's still no excuse for me acting like I did when I came home. Especially considering you basically saved my butt. You not only survived my kids for—" he squinted at the microwave clock "—nearly six hours, you obviously took excellent care of them. Not to mention going above and beyond with dinner and the cookies. So I apologize for acting like a bozo."

Finally she looked at him. "You didn't—"

"I did."

A smile teased her mouth. "Okay, maybe a little."

Silas smiled, then ground the heel of his hand into his slightly aching temple. "This single fatherhood business," he said, dropping his hand, "it's not for sissies. I remember what my brothers and I were like when we were kids and it gives me the willies, to think those two carry my genes."

"You mean you weren't always this…this…"

"Uptight?"

She lifted her hands. *Whatever.*

"No," he said on a soft laugh. "But I've gotten so used

to who I am now, I guess I've forgotten what it's like to drape cloths over the dining room table and pretend it's a fort. Used to make my mother batty. Especially the time we used her best lace tablecloth."

"I bet," Jewel said, giving the now-bare kitchen table one final swipe. "Speaking of mothers…do the boys ever see theirs?"

The unexpected question made his breath hitch in his chest. "She died in a car crash when the boys were very little," he said quietly. "Not long after our divorce."

"Ohmigosh…" Spinning around, Jewel pressed her hand to her mouth, then lowered it. "How awful," she whispered. "Do they even remember her?"

"Ollie does, a little. At least he thinks he does. But Tad was still a baby."

"Oh. That accounts for…"

Silas tensed. "For what?"

"Why you're so protective of them," she said gently. "And no, that's not a criticism, anybody in your position would be." She leaned across the counter and touched his wrist, only to remove it almost before it registered. "You're obviously a really good dad, Silas. But man—" her eyes twinkled "—you'd be a pain in the butt to live with. There," she said, surveying the much cleaner kitchen, a big smile on her face. "All fixed. Although I have to say my own place—well, Eli's, I suppose—never looks half this good. Suzy Homemaker, I'm not."

Somehow, he wasn't surprised. "I never could understand how people could live in clutter. Noah and Eli shared a room when we were teenagers—I think my mother was ready to call the HazMat team at one point."

"Sounds like Noah and me would get along great, then," she said, and he glared at her, which got another shrug. "Driving myself nuts trying to keep a place clean when it'll only get messy again simply isn't a big priority. And it's not like I've got the kind of wardrobe that needs padded hangers. Or any hangers, for that matter. I'm not *dirty,*" she said to his appalled expression, "but I'm the only one living there. Nobody comes to visit much, so if the mess doesn't bother me, who cares?"

Silas's eyes narrowed slightly. Did she even hear the loneliness weighing down her words? A loneliness he might not have even noticed if his own hadn't been all up in his face that night, whispering insane ideas in his ear, like... like maybe they could use their respective loneliness to their mutual advantage—

The idea caught him so short he actually had to grab the edge of the counter. Fortunately, Jewel had bopped back into the living room to continue straightening, so she missed it. Whew.

Silas swiveled unsteadily on the stool to watch her righting pictures, putting lamps back, as it struck him how little he actually knew about her. Except for whatever floated in Tierra Rosa's ether, like a free-for-all wireless signal. "You have any family nearby?"

"My mother's in Albuquerque, but we don't see each other much. Haven't seen my dad in years. Or my stepdads, for that matter."

"Step*dads?*"

"*Dos,*" she said holding up two fingers. "One's in Denver, the other's in Montana. Or Wyoming. I forget which. Both remarried. No, wait, the one in Denver is divorced again. I think. Can't keep track, don't really care."

Although she still periodically flashed smiles in his direction as she talked, her "chipper" was definitely fading fast. So when she bent over to gather the boys' cars—affording Silas a nice, long look at a rather appealing backside, actually—he said, "Forget it, if the boys dragged all that stuff out here, they can clean it up tomorrow before school. Besides, you're obviously exhausted."

She straightened, stretching out the muscles in her back. "And it won't drive you insane in the meantime?"

"Yes. But that's my problem, not yours."

Laughing, Jewel dumped the cars she'd already picked up, a moment before headlight beams streaked through the frosted glass insets alongside the front door. She went to gather her jacket and purse—both somewhat long in the tooth, Silas noticed—and it occurred to him she probably wasn't exactly raking it in, doing what she did. Not that he was, either, but the ends tended to overlap more than not. He pulled his wallet from his back pocket, digging out several bills.

"Here," he said, laying the cash on the counter. "This is for you."

She turned, frowning at the money as if it was foreign currency, before aiming the frown at Silas. "Excuse me?"

"For watching the kids. Cooking my dinner." When she stood there, gawking at him, he added, "If nothing else, consider it hazard pay."

Her face went bright red. "Ohmigosh! I was just helping out! Being a good neighbor! I c-can't."

She said, eying the money like it was a candy bar and she'd given up chocolate for Lent.

"And I'm sure you don't want to make me feel bad, like I took advantage of you. Please, Jewel. Take the money."

Her gaze flicked from the money to him, then back to the money. "You sure? I mean…maybe we could come to some sort of other arrangement." When his brows lifted, she said, "Like you helping me with my taxes or something."

Which, since he doubted she had pension plans and investments and the like to sort through, would probably take him ten minutes. Tops. He got up, scooped the bills off the counter and walked over to her, pressing the money into her palm, and her hand was warm and soft and strong all at once and he liked the feel of it in his way too much. Sad. "Doing your taxes is a given. Now get out of here before Patrice wakes the entire town with her horn honking."

For a long moment, their gazes tangled. Damned if he didn't like that way too much, too. Which was even sadder. "You're nuts, you know that?" she said with a little smile, stuffing the cash in her pocket. Then she yanked open his front door and fled.

No kidding, he thought, locking the door behind her, closing his eyes for a moment to embrace the peace left in her wake before yielding to the temptation to eat another cookie.

Or two.

Why Jewel'd resisted letting Silas pay her, she had no idea. Wasn't like she couldn't use it. In fact, she could squeeze two weeks' worth of groceries out of forty bucks. If she was careful. Especially since a lot of Patrice's clients paid in produce and homemade canned goods, and Patrice shared.

Although, she mused when her mentor dropped her off back at Eli's after their appointment the next morning, and she picked up the mail and there was the utilities bill sneering at her, unfortunately the gas company wasn't keen on being paid in put-by peaches, no matter how tasty they were. And she'd've still been okay if she hadn't broken her tooth last month and had had to get it capped.

She wasn't a total lamebrain, she'd socked away as much of her nurse's salary as she could, knowing she wouldn't make squat while she was doing her midwife apprenticeship. She'd had a cushion. Only the cushion turned out to be a lot thinner than she'd thought.

At least Eli was letting her stay rent-free in his house until he was ready to sell it. Otherwise she honestly didn't know what she'd do, she thought as she dug her checkbook out of her vintage Coach bag—a thrift shop score from five years ago—and flipped open the register. But alas, the Money Fairy hadn't made a stealth deposit in the middle of the night.

Shutting her eyes against the bright fall sun, Jewel stuffed the checkbook back in her purse, so distracted and disgusted and discombobulated she didn't even notice Noah standing on her roof until he called her name. She looked up, shielding her eyes, deciding she'd really be in a bad mood if the sight of all those muscles in a black T-shirt wasn't cheering her up. "Thought you said you'd send somebody over?"

"Lost the coin toss. So where's this leak again?"

"Right in the middle of the living room. And it only happens when the rain comes from the south."

Noah vanished and Jewel went inside, moping, listening to Noah's work boots stomp-stomp-stomping overhead. Then back. Then the sound of the metal extension ladder creaking as he climbed back down. A minute later, he knocked at the open door. Sitting at the small dining table in the kitchen, her head in her hands, Jewel looked up from the electric bill and its cousins, trying not to feel like a Grade A loser.

"Found the problem," Noah said. "It's not supposed to rain for the rest of the week, so I'll get back to patch it up in the next day or so. Although…" He dug his fingers into the back of his neck, shaking his head.

"Problem?"

"Yeah. Every time I come over to fix something, I find

another issue." He crossed his arms. "I doubt even Eli realizes how much work the place needs. If he wants to sell it for more than two bucks, at least."

Jewel frowned. "I'm not in any danger of the roof caving in while I sleep or anything, am I?"

"You might want to make sure your bed's under the support beam...just kidding," he said as she sagged back in the chair. "Um...you okay?"

This said in the manner of someone facing a potential bomb. Jewel almost smiled. "Other than feeling like this house? I'm fine." She wriggled her mouth back and forth a moment, then said, "Y'all wouldn't need some secretarial work done or anything, would you?" At his silence, she looked over. "What?"

"Jewel? I don't want to be mean or anything...but you really need to give this up."

"Give what up?"

"You're sweet and all, but I'm not...interested."

A laugh popped out of her mouth, only to almost immediately turn to tears. Much to her profound annoyance.

"Ah, hell, honey...I tried to let you down as easy as I knew how—"

"Oh, for heaven's sake, Noah," she said, grabbing a napkin off the table and honking into it, "I got that message loud and clear some time ago, okay? I'm not asking if you've got work to get closer to you, I'm asking because I'm broke."

Cautiously, Noah came farther into the house. "Really?"

"God's honest truth," she said on a harsh breath that released a flood of words. "The thing is, it's not like I didn't know going in how tight things were gonna be for a while until I got my license. And even then delivering babies is never gonna make me rich. And basically I'm okay with that—as long as there are thrift shops and beans and corn-bread, I'm good. Only I didn't count on breaking a tooth on a piece of hard candy, and the dentist is threatening to send the bill to collections even though I'm paying him what I can, and if I don't find a way to make some extra cash I might have to give up on being a midwife altogether. Bad enough my mother thinks it's a cockamamie idea. Oh, Noah—I can't fail, I just can't!"

She blew her nose again, then took off her glasses to wipe the lenses. "Sorry. Sometimes my emotions kinda get the best of me. What?" she said when Noah kept looking at her funny.

"Actually, I meant…" He pointed between the two of them. "You're really, um, over me?"

Wondering if the man had heard a single word she'd said, Jewel did a mental eye roll. "No offense, but worrying about starving to death kinda knocked you to the bottom of my things-to-think-about list."

"Oh. Okay. Just checking. Because I don't do—" he made air quotes "—relationships. Not in the way that most gals mean the word, at least. I have…" His forehead puck-ered. "Dalliances."

A soggy, *oh-geez,* laugh burbled from Jewel's mouth. "And you think I don't…dally?"

The puckering intensified. "Do you?"

"Guess you'll never find out now. I mean, you had your chance, but…" Her shoulders bumped. "That particular window of opportunity is now closed. But I really do need a job. So could you use some extra help? I'll do anything—scrub toilets, haul trash—I'm not proud."

Finally, he seemed to relax. "Damn, Jewel…we just hired on Luis's wife part-time. Sorry. Wish you'd said something sooner."

"No problem," she said, sighing. "Not your fault. Anyway. Thanks."

He gave her a last, lost look—men were good at that—then nodded and left, the door clicking shut behind him. With a groan Jewel let her head drop onto her folded arms, hearing her mother's voice as clear as if she'd been standing right there, going on about how silly Jewel'd been to have let Justin go, that if she'd married him she wouldn't be in this mess right now.

Maybe so, Jewel thought, lifting her head. Except for the small issue of her not wanting to get married. To Justin or anybody else. Not then, not now. Maybe not ever. But at twenty-five? No way. Not when she had all these things she wanted to do. To be.

If she sometimes yearned so much for what had kept eluding her as a child she thought she'd lose her mind, she supposed that was the trade-off for the peace that came with knowing that whatever choices she made, the only person she could hurt was herself.

And that nobody could hurt her, either.

She bet, if she had the nerve to ask him, Silas Garrett would understand where she was coming from. Shoot, ask anybody, they'd talk your ear off about his resistance to his mother's attempts to fix him up. And the look on his face when Jewel'd asked him about the boys' mother? Yeah, there was somebody who was more than happy with things the way they were, she was guessing. So if it was okay for Silas—who could probably use another set of hands and eyes to help him with those two rascals of his—to stay single, why wasn't it for her?

Never mind the bizarre ping of attraction to the man, with his soulful green eyes and killer mouth and the ten kinds of take-no-prisoners, sexy authority he exuded. A thought that, okay, got her hormones just the teensiest bit

hot and bothered. So sue her, it'd been a while. But please—
the last thing she needed in her life was an uptight, over-
protective numbers geek with borderline OCD issues.

Put like that, she probably didn't even like him. No, she
was sure she didn't. The killer mouth/soulful eyes thing
notwithstanding. And she seriously doubted he liked her.
She also seriously doubted Silas Garrett had ever been the
victim of a rogue hormone in his life. Heck, he probably
rationed the suckers, only letting them out for a half hour
on Tuesdays, Thursdays and every other Saturday.

So it was all good, right?

Blowing out a breath—and putting her rowdy hormones
in the corner—Jewel got to her feet to grab her purse and
keys to her ten-year-old Toyota Highlander with its dings
and scratches and 180,000 miles, figuring getting out of this
house would improve her mood greatly. Not to mention if
she wanted work, in all likelihood it wasn't going to come
knocking on her door, was it?

Arms folded, Silas sat on the beige corduroy couch in
his brother Eli's perpetually messy, eclectically furnished
living room, glowering at the fire in the kiva fireplace while
all around him brothers and sisters-in-law yakked, kids
raced and toddlers toddled. Every other week, at least, they
all got together for family dinner. Up until tonight that had
always been at his folks' house, but since Mom was out
of commission Eli's wife Tess had volunteered to host the
melee.

Brave woman, Silas mused as Tess shoved two action
figures and a rag doll off the overstuffed, floral chair at
a right angle to the sofa and plopped into it, her seven-
months-pregnant belly like a ripe melon underneath her
lightweight sweater. Her three-year-old daughter Julia, all
sassy dark curls and attitude, crawled up to wriggle her

butt into the space between her mother and the arm of the chair while Ollie and Julia's brother Miguel—step-cousins, classmates and cohorts in crime—chased Silas's shrieking, twenty-month-old niece Caitlin around the room. Pretending to be monsters. Or something.

"One good thing about the noise," Tess yelled over the insanity as she combed her fingers through Julia's curls, "it feels *so* good when it stops."

Silas smirked. "Does it ever?"

Humor crinkled the corners of thick-lashed dark eyes. "When the last one leaves for college?"

Silas laughed, but his heart really wasn't in it. Those eyes narrowing, Tess kissed Julia on the head and gently prodded her off the chair. "Go, torment boys," she said, then heaved herself out of the chair to drop beside Silas. The fattest, furriest cat in the world promptly jumped up in what was left of her lap, making her grunt out, "Okay, so what's up?"

Silas crossed his arms high on his chest, his forehead knotted. "You ever work when the kids are at home?"

"Hah. Not if I want to get any actual work done. Besides, I'm out showing properties more than I'm in, anyway. I owe my babysitter my life."

His eyes cut to hers. Purring madly, the cat stretched out one paw to rest it on Silas's arm. "She wouldn't have any openings, would she?"

Tess's brow creased in reply. "No luck with the day care?"

Tad bellowed behind him, making him flinch. "One place has a possible opening in October. *Mid*-October. *Possible* being the key word here."

"Donna should be okay by then—"

"After raising the four of us, she wants her life back."

"Oh."

"Yeah. *Oh.* Can't say as I blame her."

Tess's gaze shifted to her mother-in-law, holding court on the loveseat across the room, clearly enjoying the hell out of playing Queen Bee. "No," Tess sighed out. "I wouldn't blame her, either. I thought my two were energy suckers, but yours have mine beat by a mile."

"Thanks."

"Hey…maybe Rachel could fill in? She could probably use the extra bucks—"

"Did somebody say extra bucks?" his youngest sister-in-law said, her long, dark hair streaked with burgundy, her long, legginged legs ending in a pair of those dumb, fat suede boots. Pink ones, no less.

"I need a babysitter—"

Lime green fingernails flashed as Rach's hand shot up. "Sorry, Si, but I'm doing well to handle this one," she said, bouncing pudgy Caiti on her hip, "and school as it is. I'd really like to help, but I'm majorly slammed this semester." She wrinkled her pierced nose. "We still good?"

"Of course, I understand completely." Silas slumped forward, holding his head, as she strode off. "I'm doomed."

"Why are you doomed?" Noah said, commandeering the chair Tess had just vacated and simultaneously digging into a plate of leftovers. Because clearly the first two helpings weren't enough.

Tess gave Silas's back a sympathetic pat. "Sweetie can't find anybody to watch the boys."

"Yeah," Noah said, chewing, "that's the problem with kids, the way somebody always has to watch 'em." He swallowed, pointing his fork at Silas. "A problem, you will note, I do not have."

"Jerk," Silas muttered without heat, since it was no secret the dude would kill for his nieces and nephews, even if the idea of having his own kids gave him hives.

A piece of chicken vanished into his brother's mouth. "What about Jewel?"

Silas's head snapped up. "Jewel?"

"Yeah. She said she's got some medical bills or something—she was kind of rambling, I didn't quite get all of it—and she's pretty desperate for some part-time work. Even asked me if we could use her over at the shop. Hey," he said to Silas's frown, "you said yourself she was great with the boys. And they like her, right? So why not? You need a sitter, she needs a job…" He shrugged those big shoulders of his. "Sounds like a win-win to me—"

"What it sounds like, is a disaster in the making."

Noah and Tess exchanged a glance before Noah met Silas's gaze again. "Be-cause…?"

Where would they like him to start? "What if she has to go on a call while she's got the kids? What then?"

"Oh, between all of us," Tess said, far too enthusiastically, "I'm sure we could fill in any gaps. I'm with Noah—it sounds like a perfect plan to me."

Yeah. The perfect plan from hell.

"Uh-oh," Noah said. "He's got that look on his face."

Silas glared at him. "What look?"

"The I-don't-wanna look. Never mind there's not one good reason why this isn't a good idea. For cripe's sake, she's a nurse, she knows CPR and stuff. And she cooks—"

"Ow!" Silas said when Tess cuffed the back of his head. "What the—?"

"Hell, if you don't hire her, I will. So call her. Before somebody else snatches her up."

His mouth open to protest, Silas shut it again. Because Tess was right—maybe the thought of having Jewel in his house every day gave him the heebie-jeebies, but she could probably find a temporary nanny position in a heartbeat, if not here, in Santa Fe or Taos. And he was desperate.

Not so desperate, however, that he couldn't wait to call until he got home, since for damn sure he didn't need an audience to add to his humiliation.

So, an hour later, the boys bellowing and sloshing blissfully in the tub, Silas ducked back into their room to make the call, so focused on them through the door he almost forgot who he was calling until she said, "Silas?" in a voice far raspier than he remembered, or expected, or wanted, or needed, and for a moment he was torn between praying she'd say yes and fervently hoping somebody else *would* snatch her up.

Thereby saving him from a fate worse than death.

Chapter Three

It took Jewel so long to process Silas's number on the display that her voice mail nearly clicked in before she answered. "Uh...hello—?"

"Noah says you're looking for work?"

Three thoughts zipped through simultaneously. One, that warp-speed Internet connection had nothing on Tierra Rosa's gossip mill, especially when major chunks of the mill were related to each other; two, that he sounded about as thrilled about making this call as he would have making an appointment for one of *those* exams; and three, *Wow. Deep voice.*

"Um...yeah? You know of something?"

He sighed. The kind of sigh that precedes bad news. "Turns out there are no day-care openings, anywhere. At least not for several weeks. Meaning I need a part-time nanny. And the boys like you. So. You want the job?"

Oh, no. Nononononono. Because that little ping of

awareness she'd thought a onetime thing? Yeah, well… apparently not. She tried—oh, how she tried—to send her hormones back into time-out, but since there was only one of her and five quadrillion of them…

"Gee, Silas, I don't know. Um…what if I get called out on a birth?"

"But how often does that happen? Couple times a month?"

Her mouth twisted. "Maybe. But there's prenatal appointments, and follow-up visits…"

"Even three days a week would work. Or just in the afternoons. Or mornings, whatever works for you." Silence. "I'm really, really in a bind."

"You must be to ask me."

More silence. "The good news is, we'd rarely be around each other."

"So you *don't* like me."

"Whatever gave you that idea—?"

"Silas. Please."

Somehow, she imagined him removing his glasses, rubbing his eyes. The hormones moaned.

Shut. Up.

"I think it's safe to say—" he exhaled into the phone "—that we have…different ways of approaching life. But that's neither here nor there. Look, I'll pay you whatever… whatever you think is fair. Name your price."

Visions of paid bills and maybe a new pair of hiking boots danced in her head. Cautiously she tossed out a figure, Silas said, "Done," and Jewel sucked in a breath. "And like I said," he added, "it's only temporary. Until October. So what kind of schedule would work for you?"

"Um…if you don't mind being flexible, why don't we take it day by day—?"

"Works for me. Can you start tomorrow?"

"Uh, yeah…sure—"

"Then how about I swing by your place about eight-thirty to give you a set of keys to the house? And instructions?"

"I guess. We don't have any appointments tomorrow, so—"

"Great. See you then."

Instructions, right, Jewel thought through the mild dizziness as she set her phone back on the counter. No doubt annotated and color coded. Like those scary Supernanny charts.

Her hormones scrambled for cover.

"Dad-*dy!* Where *are* you?"

Kids. Right.

Still clutching his phone, Silas walked back into the bathroom where his children—irrefutable evidence of his life having once included sex—had apparently decided why use a tiny squirt of shampoo when half the bottle was so much better? Or—he picked up the weightless plastic shell from the middle of the bathmat—the entire bottle. However, given the condition Silas and his brothers used to leave the bathroom in after their baths when they were kids, he was grateful most of the water was actually still in the tub.

"Look at Tad's hair!" Ollie said, giggling and pointing to the Marge Simpson 'do atop his youngest son's head. Ollie, however, had gone more Marie Antoinette. All he needed was one of his plastic boats on top to complete the look.

Giving Silas a big, dimpled grin, Tad scooped up a mountain of froth. "We made bubbles!"

"So I see," Silas said, sinking onto the covered toilet lid and thinking, *God, I love these kids,* his heart seizing up with a random attack of the what-might-have-beens. At least they didn't happen as often as they did in the beginning.

But they still came, sneaking up on him like ninjas in the middle of the night. Or like now, when the thought of entrusting them to some ponytailed, raspy-voiced, braless weirdo was making his brain hurt.

Figuring the suds made soaping them up redundant, Silas rolled up his shirt sleeves and turned on the handheld shower, a move that got a pair of "Awwww...not yets!"

"You want me to read?" he said as Marge, then Marie, dissolved into foamy streaks slithering down the boys' chests. "Then you have to get out of the tub now." Doughboy appeared at the open doorway, took one look at the Torture Weapon in Silas's hand and backed out again. "And anyway," he said, wrapping up each boy in turn like little mummies in their bath sheets, "I've got news." He grabbed Tad to rub his curls mostly dry with a hand towel. "Jewel's agreed to be your nanny."

"Re-re-really?" Ollie said as Silas attacked his wet head, his grin enormous when he resurfaced, a blond porcupine pumping his fist. "Yes!"

"Yes!" Tad echoed, his still-damp curls bobbing as he, too, pumped his fist so hard he lost his towel. Then naturally both boys dissolved into giggles because, you know, life was go-*ood*.

Smiling, grateful, Silas hauled them both into his arms—was there anything better in the whole wide world than freshly bathed little boys?—and down the hall to their room, where he read three books and tucked them in with hugs and kisses and tried very, very hard not to think about Jewel Jasper's voice.

Which he'd be hearing again in...less than twelve hours.

Hell.

* * *

The doorbell rang precisely at eight-thirty the next morning.

Waking Jewel up.

Muttering not-nice words, she fought her way out of the tangled covers—she'd always been a thrasher, had been told sharing a bed with her was like trying to sleep in a blender—yanking on her shorty robe as she lurched toward the front door.

The bell rang again. As did her cell phone.

She glanced at the display. Oh, joy.

"'Lo," she croaked as she tugged open the front door, assuming it'd be Silas on the other side and not an escaped convict. Or worse, somebody trying to save her soul. *Got it in one,* she thought as, nodding to Silas to come in, she pointed to the phone and mouthed, "My mother."

"Oh, sugar, I'm so glad I got you…." Hearing the tears in her mother's voice, Jewel squeezed shut her eyes, only to realize when she opened them again that Silas was staring at the life-size pelvis complete with embryo and placenta sitting on the banged-up coffee table she'd picked up for next-to-nothing at a yard sale when she'd moved into the house. She shoved the front door closed with her bare foot, her mother's "Monty broke up with me!" knifing through her morning groggies as she padded into the living room.

"Oh…I'm so sorry," she said, thinking, *Who the heck is Monty?* On her way to the kitchen she poked Silas in the arm, distracting him from the pelvis. "Coffee?"

"Uh…sure," he said, distracting Mama from Monty. For the moment.

"Honey? Who are you talking to?"

"A friend," Jewel said, shrugging at Silas's lifted eyebrows before yanking open the fridge for the Folgers, briefly considering snorting it instead of waiting for it to brew.

"Don't you try to fool me, young lady, that was a man's voice!"

"Nothin' gets past you, huh?" Jewel said, carting the coffee over to the coffee maker, remembering too late when she reached up into the cupboard for the filters that she wasn't wearing anything under the robe. Oops. "I can have men friends, Mama." Although having them ogle her butt wasn't on the list this morning. "Listen, I have to go, but how's about I come down and go to lunch with you or something on Saturday? Cheer you up?"

"Oh…not today?"

Jewel sighed. Much as she truly loved her mother, all she wanted was for the woman to grow up. To *be* her mother and not that clingy chick in high school who tells everybody she's your BFF when she's not.

To give Jewel a chance to do some growing up of her own.

"I'd love to, Mama, really, but my day's already full. But hey—why don't you go shopping? You know that always makes you feel better." For at least twenty minutes.

"Well…I suppose I could." A delicate sniff sounded in Jewel's ear. "But it'd be so much more fun with you along."

At one point, that had been true enough. For Jewel, anyway. Nobody knew her way around a mall better than her mother, even if Mama was always trying to buy Jewel prissy, girly-girl things she'd never wear. "I know, but I can't today. I'll call you later, how's that?"

After promising her mother she'd call as soon as she could, Jewel pocketed her cell and shut her eyes again, willing the coffee aroma into her veins. As usual the conversation was ripping her in two: she could be what her mother wanted her to be, or what Jewel needed to be, but not both. And the endless tug-of-war was making her bonkers.

Still, self-preservation kept her heels dug in and her bleeding hands tight on that rope, boy…or risk toppling right over into the Aching Void of Need she'd had to haul Kathryn DuBois out of more times than she could count, when yet another relationship fizzled out on her. On them both, actually, since losing three "daddies" and any number of also-rans hadn't done Jewel any favors, either.

But if nothing else she'd learned from her mother's example, having seen first-hand the vicious cycle of hope and heartbreak that were part and parcel of letting "love" blind you to reality. Hence her resolve to never let anybody do to her what so many had done to her mother.

Besides, if she didn't stay strong, who'd take care of Mama?

"Let me guess," Silas said behind her, making her jump. Because somehow she'd forgotten he was there. "I woke you."

Jewel made sure she was smiling before she turned. "Only because I slept through my alarm." She peered behind him. "You lose somebody?"

"The kids? Like there was any way we could talk with them around. Anyway, Ollie's in school already. I left Tad at the shop with Noah. And my dad. And everybody else. One kid, a half-dozen sets of eyes…should work out just about right." Silas folded his arms over his chest. Doing the Stern Look thing. On him, it worked. As did the gray, geometric-patterned sweater and jeans. Geek chic. "You do that often? Sleep through your alarm?"

Jewel's stomach growled, reminding her of the vast void within. "No, actually," she said, opening another cupboard door for oatmeal. "But I got called out unexpectedly last night with a mother having false labor. She didn't settle down—" she yawned "—until nearly five." The oatmeal dumped into a bowl with milk, she set it in the microwave and edged toward the fridge. "Want some eggs with your coffee?"

"Already ate. Thanks."

"Whatever. I'm starving." She cracked three eggs into a bowl, dumped two pieces of what her mother called "bird seed" bread into the toaster. "But don't you worry," she said, banging a skillet onto the old gas stove, "that was a one-off. My sleeping in, I mean. Normally I'm up at like six, raring to go. I have a lot of energy, which you may have noticed."

But she doubted he'd heard her, since when she turned he was frowning at the disaster of a living room with its re-re-recycled furniture, littered with DVDs and textbooks and clothing that had wandered out of her closet and hadn't yet found its way back, not to mention the dozen bulging, partially ripped garbage bags of kids' and baby clothes and toys the church ladies had left for her to pass along to some of her and Patrice's needier clients. The pelvis. Then his gaze drifted back to her, those green eyes positively teeming with questions.

And something else, something that sent little flickers of heat hoppity-skipping through her blood. Good thing, then—*really* good thing—she didn't have to worry about pesky things like him maybe coming on to her. Because, alas, she was only human. And kinda, um, *lonely,* truth be told. As was Silas, she'd bet the farm.

Which could present a problem. Because while Jewel was not into sharing her body with all and sundry, she did have to admit to a certain fondness for sex, dimly remembered though that might be. Hence the hormones, which even now were whispering how little stoking it would take to go from flickers to raging conflagration.

Little creeps.

"Maybe you should get dressed," Silas said softly, taking the bowl of beaten eggs from her, and she thought, *Don't look at the mouth,* even as she noticed how turned down that mouth was at the corners. Disapproving and whatnot. "Before somebody sees us through the window—" he nodded toward the curtainless kitchen window facing the street "—and gets the wrong idea."

Oh.

Her cheeks flaming, Jewel fled, feeling like a scolded little girl.

Which went a long way toward damping those flickers, boy. Yes, indeedy.

Silas beat those eggs as if his salvation depended on it.

Since his reaction to Jewel was making him feel close enough to perv status to ratchet the discomfort level up to, oh, about a million-point-two.

Even though there was no reason it should. Okay fine, so a brief glimpse of her bare bottom—hell, if he'd blinked he would've missed it—when she'd lifted her arms had fired a jet or two. Perfectly natural. And inevitable, frankly, considering how long it'd been since those particular jets had fired.

It was who the jets were firing for that had him all shook up.

Why hadn't he blinked? Why?

Silas set the bowl of eggs on the counter—no point scrambling them until she returned, they'd only get cold— and wandered back into the living room, which could only be called a wreck. Gal hadn't been kidding about her housekeeping skills. Or lack thereof. Scrupulously avoiding the model of the female innards on the coffee table, he instead found himself checking out the dozen or so videos scattered beside it.

Big mistake.

Orgasmic Birth?

"Snooping?" Jewel said from the other side of the room, making him spin around to see she'd buried all jet-firing attributes beneath a too-big, zipped-to-the-neck hoodie and a pair of holey jeans. Hair back. Face bare.

Eyes wary.

Aaaand there went the protective mode again.

Better than perv mode. Right?

Maybe. Maybe not.

"Of course not—"

"Oh, that's the one in the player now," she said, nodding at the case. Still in his hand. *Busted*. He lifted it, coherent speech beyond him. She grinned, effectively disabling the protective mode. "It's excellent, you should give it a look-see sometime. Eggs ready yet?"

"No, sorry…" Silas dropped the case—setting off a clattering DVD avalanche which he had to stop and clean up—before following her back to the kitchen. "Didn't want 'em to get cold," he said, turning the flame on underneath the cheapo skillet.

"I can do that—"

"No, it's okay, you sit." *So I don't have to look at you.*

She got her oatmeal out of the microwave, stirred in a generous pat of butter and like half a cup of syrup of some kind. Good Lord. "You sure—?"

"Yes," Silas said.

So she sat, and he scrambled—the eggs, his brain, whatever—a minute later sliding the plate with eggs and toast in front of her at the chewed-up dining table. Her gaze met his for a nanosecond then skittered away, yanking her usual exuberance along with it. Huh.

"Thanks," she said, pushing her glasses up on her nose, and it occurred to him she didn't see herself as sexy. Which was not his problem. No, his problem was *him* seeing her as sexy.

"Can't remember the last time anybody made me breakfast," she said, not looking at him as she scraped the last bit of oatmeal from the bowl and dived into the toast and eggs.

Silas poured himself a cup of coffee, leaning up against her counter to drink it while she ate. And ate, and ate. Where on earth she put it all, he couldn't begin to guess.

"Your mother okay?" he asked, more out of politeness than curiosity. Heaven knew he had enough issues with his own mother, he sure as heck didn't want or need to hear about anyone else's.

After staring at him a moment too long, Jewel shoved her cheerfulness back out front, like a pushy mama making little Johnny sing for the folks. "Oh, she'll be fine," she said with a wave of her hand and a let's-not-go-there smile. "She's real good at landing on her feet. In more ways than one. So…" Her eggs polished off, she crammed the last bite of toast into her mouth and brushed off her hands. "What all do I need to know about the boys?"

And would somebody explain to him, considering he was only being polite to begin with, why the brush-off stung? Not a lot, but enough to make him wonder.

He pulled a list of instructions and emergency phone numbers from his back pocket and unfolded it, setting it in front of her. Still chewing, she quickly read it, then glanced up at him, her eyes glittering with amusement behind her glasses. *Like snow in shadow,* he thought, then mentally slapped himself.

"Why don't you just send 'em to military school and be done with it?"

Silas bristled. "I love my kids, Jewel. And I take my fathering responsibilities very seriously."

"Well, of course you do! I don't mean…" After checking for a clean spot on her napkin, she yanked off her glasses to clean them. "Okay, I was only trying to make light of the moment, but…" The glasses shoved back on, she huffed out, "My mouth has this bad habit of spitting out random inappropriateness when I least expect it. I apologize."

This said eye-to-eye. Earnestly. Sincerely.

"And anyway, this—" she lifted the list, thankfully oblivious to the sudden, random buzzing in Silas's head "—isn't near as bad as I expected. Considering the boys', um, high energy level."

The buzzing faded. For which Silas was even more thankful. "The phrase 'holy terrors' has been bandied about a time or six."

Jewel's eyes popped wide enough for him to see gold flecks in the dusky blue irises. "They are not *terrors!* By any stretch of the imagination! And whoever would say such a thing…" Her mouth pulled flat, she shook her head. "Honestly. Some people need their brains washed out. They're just little *boys,* for crying out loud," she said, her fervor pinking her cheeks and making her eyes bluer, and *Damn, she's beautiful* smacked Silas right between the eyes. Hell.

"Sounds like you've had experience with little boys," he said, and her indignation melted into a chuckle.

"You couldn't tell?" Then she flicked her hand: *Never mind.* "Yeah, I do. When my mother married my stepfather—my second one, I mean—my stepbrother was a toddler. I was eleven, and ohmigosh, I thought Aaron was the cutest thing ever. I adored him, took him everywhere, played dress-up with him—you can wipe that look off your face, your boys are safe, I outgrew that phase years ago—even let him sleep in my bed with me. 'Course," she said with a crooked little grin, "the older he got the more I decided he was a pain in the posterior, but I still loved him. Still do," she added softly. "God, I miss that kid."

Again, with the sincerity. Still, with the buzzing. "Where is he now?"

"Denver." Her eyes lowered again to the list, although Silas guessed she wasn't seeing it. "Keith—that's his dad— and Mama split up when I was sixteen. Aaron and I still talk, every couple of weeks or so. Mostly I follow him on MySpace, although he's lousy about updating his page. I do, however, send him horribly embarrassing birthday and Christmas presents..."

Silas could have sworn her hand shook slightly before she fisted it, then looked back up at him, her mouth hiked up again on one side. "So I know all about little boys." A short, light laugh *hmmphed* through her nose. "Trust me, after Aaron? There's no stunt your two can pull I haven't seen a dozen times."

For a good couple of seconds, Silas wrestled with the impulse to ask questions he had no right to ask. Questions that would lead places he doubted either of them wished to visit. Fortunately, the impulse faded and he asked, "I often work at home—that a problem for you?"

Her brow crinkled. "No. Why should it be?"

"Because I'm not one of those blessed souls who can work with kids racing and tearing around the house. I don't expect absolute silence," he said when her frown deepened, "only that you keep them from crashing into the office every ten minutes when I'm working."

"Understood. Although..." The frown relaxed into something he couldn't quite define. "It must be hard on all of you, you being there, but not."

"Believe me, I'd much rather hang out with my kids than

stare at spreadsheets. But it's those spreadsheets that keep a roof over their heads."

"Yeah, I hear ya," she sighed out, then gave a sharp nod. "I promise, I'll do my best to keep the boys occupied while you're working. Just remember—" mischief curved her mouth, danced in her eyes, and Silas suddenly wanted to dance with her, naked in the pale moonlight "—what you don't know won't hurt you."

"That's what I'm afraid of." That, and the wanting to dance naked in the moonlight thing. Because that was crazy, *she* was crazy, and Silas didn't do crazy. "Tad, especially, will test you with every breath he takes."

"I'm sure. But don't you worry, I can take anything he can dish out. And anyway, if he doesn't test his limits—" she rose to carry her dishes to the sink "—how's he ever gonna find out what those limits are?"

"I'm thinking that's not his decision to make," Silas said, reasserting his control over…everything. "Which means you and I better agree on some boundaries."

Rinsing her dishes, she tossed him another mischief-riddled grin over her shoulder. "Like your folks set for you and your brothers?"

"They set 'em, sure. We kept barreling right past 'em."

Jewel grabbed a dish towel off the cabinet knob under the sink and turned, drying her hands, that damned impish smile still twinkling at him. Unnerving him. "You did hear what you just said, right?"

"You could at least humor me, you know."

The towel replaced, she giggled, then stuffed her hands in her hoodie's pockets. "I've heard the stories. You guys were legendary, huh?"

"Some of us still are," he muttered, earning him another laugh.

"So you'll do anything to prevent history from repeating

itself. Got it. I mean, good luck with that and all, but I'm only the hired help. Whatever rules you set, I'll abide by 'em. Promise. Can't promise that I won't bend 'em every now and again, though."

"Jewel—" Silas sighed. "Oh. You're messing with me again."

"Now you're catching on," she said, grabbing her car keys—and the list—and heading out. "Well, let's get going—you've got work to do. And for heaven's sake, a woodworking shop is no place for a four-year-old—whatever were you *thinking?*"

Good question, Silas thought as he followed her, mesmerized by her gleaming, bouncing ponytail in the morning sun.

Chapter Four

Like many northern New Mexican villages, tiny Tierra Rosa blurred into the mountainous countryside beyond its borders. Silas's adobe, clinging to the outskirts on one of the last named streets, had probably started out life as a single-room farmhouse a century or more ago, gradually expanding like a multiplying cell as successive generations added bedrooms, indoor plumbing, a working kitchen. A flagstone patio with a built-in firepit. Even so, the multiple—and not always successful—attempts at modernization only added to its kitschy charm.

Two words Jewel never in her wildest dreams would have associated with Silas Garrett.

Now—after installing the booster seats his parents usually kept in their SUV into Jewel's—Silas had gone off to save the world from incorrectly added numbers and Jewel, Tad and Doughboy were in Silas's backyard, scouting out the many holes Doughboy had thoughtfully already provided for little boys looking for a place to bury deceased hamsters, mice or—in this case—goldfish.

"You sure you're warm enough?" she called out to Tad, who was darting from spot to spot, baggied fish in hand.

"Uh-huh. How 'bout over there?" The fish, mercifully oblivious, bungeed up, then dropped as Tad pointed with it. So much for respect for the dead.

"Looks good to me."

Huddled against the chilly breeze, Jewel carefully navigated rocks and tree roots and a dozen more holes on her way over. Despite the obstacle course, it was a nice yard, big, shaded by an enormous, gold-splashed mulberry tree—just begging for a tree house, if you asked her—in one corner, the other taken over by one of those big wooden swing and play sets. Beyond the tall cedar plank fence bordering the space, live oaks and dusky, prickly piñons sparkled and swayed, teasing little boys—and young women who chafed at being fenced in—to come explore.

Not that she didn't understand that you couldn't simply let babies wander off into the woods unsupervised. But the fence seemed so…forbidding. So solid. So be-careful-bad-things-might-happen-*if*.

Man, she hated that "if."

"You sure you don't want to wait until your daddy gets home?" Jewel asked, catching up to the boy as he solemnly laid the fish in the hole farthest from the house. Closest to the fence. Like maybe it could swim to the other side. Blond curls quivered as he shook his head, then turned those great big, pine-colored eyes on her, reminding her so much of her step-brother at that age her heart squeezed.

"Daddy gets all weird when people talk about dead stuff."

He stood, dusting off his hands, and Jewel wondered if

the kid had missed the memo that he was only four. Honest to Pete.

Jewel took up one of the two spades they'd carted over from the small shed a few feet away and started shoveling dirt back into the hole, provoking a pang of misgiving that the fish would be encased for all eternity in his plastic shroud. "Weird, how?"

"Like he doesn't know what to say. No, Doughboy!" Tad grabbed the stocky dog around the chest—sort of—and gave him an ineffectual shove away from the hole. "Leave it alone!"

Jowls quivering, the dog trudged right back of course, but he seemed more respectful this time, plopping down with his head between his chunky paws. Undoubtedly biding his time until he could dig the corpse up again, thereby putting certain ecological issues to rest. The hole filled, Tad leaned back on his knees and rubbed his nose, smearing dirt across his face. "You think Harvey's in heaven?"

Jewel squatted beside him. "I don't see why not. In fact, I bet he's swimming around in this big, beautiful, sunny pond in God's garden—"

"Does he have wings?"

"Oh. I'm no expert, sugarpie, but I'm guessing not—"

"Do you think Mama's in heaven? Watching me and Ollie?"

Jewel stared at the back of Tad's head as he leaned forward again to smooth the dirt over the tiny grave. Silly her, thinking the hardest thing about the job would be whether to make peanut butter or tuna sandwiches for lunch. She touched his hair. "You know, maybe that's something you should ask your daddy."

"I did. Lotsa times." Tad scooped up a trowel full of extra dirt, letting it dribble onto the ground. "He always finds something else to talk about."

Jewel remembered how she'd pestered her mother half to death about her father when she was about Tad's age, finally able to ask questions at four she hadn't been able to at two. She supposed that's what was happening with Tad, only now ready to deal with his mama's death. However, it was up to Tad's daddy to dole out answers. Not her.

Except before she could ask if he'd like her to say something to Silas, cutie patootie jumped up, swiping his filthy hands across his butt, then his nose. "I'm hungry. Can you make more cookies? Then can we give the dog a bath after lunch? 'Cuz he stinks." He put his grubby hand in hers and led her back toward the house, wriggling and skipping and jumping to the point where he practically yanked her arm out of the socket. "An' then c'n we play Secret City again? That was *so* fun!"

"Yes to the cookies—although we'll probably have to go to the store first, I doubt there's anything to make 'em with—no to the dog and we'll see about Secret City. Your daddy got kinda…upset when we played it before."

"But he won't find out if we get it all cleaned up before he gets home. Right?"

Then the kid grinned, and she was lost. Laughing, she grabbed him around the waist to tickle him, reveling in his squealing laughter and figuring what old stick-in-the-mud Silas didn't know wouldn't hurt him.

"Look sharp!"

Silas barely looked up in time to catch the wrapped burrito his brother Eli tossed across the desk, the cardboard box in his other hand holding three drinks large enough to give everybody's kidneys a good workout the rest of the day. The drinks set on the desk, Eli plucked off his ball cap, raked a banged-up hand through his too-long brown hair and grabbed his own burrito from the box.

"We may as well get started. Noah'll be along in a minute, he's over patching up my old roof."

"And Dad?"

"Gone home to see how Mama's getting on," Eli said, his butt not even making contact with one of the two chairs on the other side of the desk before he'd chomped off a quarter of the burrito. Blue, their father's old heeler, wriggled and whined in anticipation of whatever handouts he might get, getting his snout shoved out of Eli's lap for his efforts. "You know how he worries."

A trait Silas had apparently inherited, he thought as he rose from his own chair, tugging his jacket off the back.

"And where do you think you're going?" Eli mumbled around a full mouth.

"Home. It's Tad's and Jewel's first day together. I should see how things are going—"

"Did anybody call and say there was a problem?" Eli said, licking his greasy fingers. Evangelista's burritos were not for the fainthearted.

"No, but—"

"Then sit your rear back down, you ain't going nowhere."

Silas glared at his younger brother. "You got a problem with me at least calling to see how they're doing?"

"No. But Jewel might. *Sit*."

"Since when do you get to order me around?"

"Since you started acting like a pea-brain about your kids."

"And you being a stepdad for five minutes doesn't make you an instant authority on fatherhood."

Eli gave Silas a hard look for a moment before swallowing. "No. It doesn't. And it's not like I don't understand where you're coming from, that there's always this shadow in the back of your brain that something might happen.

Before Tess told me she was pregnant I had no idea you could feel so excited and so terrified at the same time. But seems like you've gotten even more skittish about the boys over the last little while than you were right after the accident. You keep that up," he said, taking another bite of his lunch, "and you're gonna push yourself over the edge. Not to mention everybody else."

They glared at each other for a moment before, on a heavy sigh, Silas dropped back into the chair and unwrapped the burrito he didn't feel much like eating. "Sorry. It's just…" The pungent tang of *carne adovada* made his mouth water anyway. "The bigger they get the more they remind me of you and Noah. Then I remember some of the pranks the two of you pulled on me and my blood goes cold."

Eli snorted. "You do realize most of those were in retaliation for the crap *you* pulled on us, right?"

"Uh, sorry, but I wasn't even around that time you goons jumped onto the trampoline from the roof."

"Oh, come on, we were fine. Noah didn't even have a concussion."

Silas almost laughed, then sighed. "It was like we were on a mission to make our folks' lives a living hell."

"And yet, they still love us. Just like we'll still love our kids. You're thinking too hard, Si. Give it a rest—"

"He at it again?" Noah said as came in and swiped a burrito and drink from the box. Sensing new opportunities, Blue immediately switched loyalties.

"Had to stop him from going to check on Jewel and Tad."

"Bro," Noah said, and Silas jabbed a finger in his direction.

"*You* do not get a say in this, Mr. Everybody-else-is-having-kids-so-I-don't-gotta."

After loudly crumpling the burrito wrapping and lobbing it into the wastebasket, Noah sprawled on the old futon against the far wall. Scowling, he kneed the dog out of his way, only to immediately hand him a piece of steak from his burrito. "And if Mom's laying a guilt trip on me doesn't work, for damn sure *you* don't have a shot." He stuffed another chunk of meat into his mouth. "Fatherhood's not in the cards for me. Deal."

"I'm not arguing with your choice, bonehead. I'm arguing with your right to horn in on how I'm doing my job."

Clearly unperturbed, Noah shrugged, then waved the half eaten burrito in their brother's direction. "You probably won't like what I've got to say, either."

Eli's brows dipped. "Oh?"

"Yeah. That roof is a lot worse than I first thought. All that snow we got last winter leaked right through the barrier paper, did a real number on the wood underneath."

"Hell." Eli's brows dipped. "You sure?"

"Kinda got my first clue when my foot went through this morning. We could patch it, but if you're planning on selling?" He took another bite, shaking his head. "It'd never pass inspection like that. Whole thing needs to be replaced, if you want my opinion. And before winter sets in, or it's only gonna get a lot worse. The good news is, I'll do it for cost."

"Jerk," Eli said, tossing his crushed, supposedly empty soda cup at his brother. Laughing, Noah caught it and threw it back, making the dog bark.

Wiping soda drops off his arms, Silas frowned "What about Jewel? Can she stay there while you're working?"

Noah pulled a face. "I sure wouldn't want to, if I were her."

"How long are we talking?"

"Depending on how bad it is, if the weather cooperates...a

week? Maybe two? Maybe she could stay up at the house? I'm sure the folks wouldn't mind."

"No room," Eli said, crossing his arms. "Aunt Marie's there helping out, remember? And Dad moved his car collection into our old room. What about your spare room, Si?"

Silas's eyes jerked to his brother's. "You're not serious?"

"Well, yeah. I mean, if she can't find someplace else, why not?"

"It's only for a week," Noah put in. "Two at the most. Probably not even. And anyway, only as a last resort, right?"

Except, when Silas didn't respond fast enough, he caught the brothers' shared glance, followed by the sly, no-good grin creeping across Noah's face.

"Bunny rabbit got you scared?" Noah said, and Eli chuckled, and Silas briefly recalled—with a small thrill of satisfaction—the time he'd put garden snakes in their beds and made them both scream like girls.

Ah, those were the days.

"No," Silas said, grabbing Blue's collar to jerk him out of the trash before he got Noah's wrapper. "And don't you two have work to do?"

"Sure thing—"

"Yeah, guess we're done here."

Then they left, still chuckling, making Silas wonder, once again, why, *why* his parents hadn't stopped at one.

"You're right, sweetie, that sucks," Jewel said to her cell phone, propped on the counter, as she turned down the heat under the pot of rice on the stove. True, Silas hadn't asked her to make dinner, but it wasn't like tossing the pork and fixings into the crock pot earlier had been any big deal.

"Seriously," her stepbrother rumbled. Holy moly, who turned up the bass? "It's like every time I turn around Dad's got somebody new. Why can't it ever be just the two of us?"

An outburst of laughter from the boys' room, where in all likelihood they were plotting world domination, sent Jewel closer so she could hear better. She'd already learned not to leave them alone for longer than five minutes or there would be hell to pay. By the middle of the afternoon Tad had already managed to wipe out half her brain cells; his brother handily took care of the rest within fifteen minutes of his return from school.

"Jewel? You listening to me?"

"Sorry—" she pulled her head back into the kitchen "—I'm a little distracted—"

"And this last one's a real bitch!"

"Aaron!"

"No lie, she really is. I heard her saying it was too bad my real mom wasn't still alive so Dad could send me back to her."

Jewel's heart cracked in two. For all her mother's faults, Kathryn would've kicked to the curb any man who'd tried to make her choose between him and Jewel. Mama might not be exactly the strongest nail in the bin, but she was nothing if not loyal.

"Oh, honey…I'm so sorry. But look on the bright side—this one probably won't last, either."

A sigh came through the phone. "Yeah. I know." He paused. "I sure wish I could come live with you—"

"And we've been all through this, sweetie. I love you to bits, you know that, but I'm not in any position to take care of a fifteen-year-old boy—"

"But you wouldn't have to take care of me! You wouldn't!

I even get myself ready for school, pack my own lunch and everything! Please?"

"Honey…no. First off, I doubt your dad would be on board with that. And second, I simply can't be responsible for you. And I would be, whether you think so or not. Besides, are you sure maybe you didn't misinterpret what that woman said—?"

"You're not here, Jewel, you don't see…" She could hear him fight tears; her own eyes stung in response. "It's like Dad doesn't know what to do with me or something. Like I'm gum on his shoe he can't get off."

Oh, Lord—the child was gonna burn her heart right out of her body, and that was the truth. "Tell you what," she said as she heard the front door open, Silas's keys clatter into the metal dish on the hall table. "Maybe you can come visit for Thanksgiving. You, me, a twenty-pound turkey and football until your eyes fall out. How's that sound?"

"And your mom, right?"

"I suppose. Who knows? But…you'd be okay with that?"

"Sure. I mean, yeah, Kathryn's a little weird, but at least she was always nice to me. When she was around, anyway." He paused. "You really mean it? About me coming for Thanksgiving?"

"Of course I do! If it's okay with Keith, why not?" She signaled to the frowning Silas she'd only be a sec. She also told herself he only looked that good on account of her spending the entire day with people who barely came up to her hip, but she knew that was a bold-faced lie. "I gotta go now, but we'll talk again later, okay? Love you, kiddo. My stepbrother," she said to The Scowl when she disconnected the call. "I'm gathering my ex-stepfather is being a butt."

Catching sight of the plate of oatmeal cookies, Silas slid onto a barstool in front of them. "Sorry to hear it," he said, shoving a cookie into his mouth and making a big old mess all over the counter.

Jewel shrugged, then pulled two glasses and a pair of plastic tumblers from the cupboard, briefly contemplating whether to bring up Tad's needing to talk about his mom before deciding, no, it wasn't her place. Not yet, at least. Instead she said, "You know that mulberry out back? Those low branches are perfect for a tree house. And the kids would love it, right?"

"Yeah, I suppose," Silas said, like he was only half listening. Jewel turned to see him sweeping cookie crumbs into his palm, obviously avoiding eye contact.

"Silas? Is something wrong?"

The crumbs deposited into a napkin, he rubbed his fingers together, then finally met her gaze. "Noah says the roof on Eli's house is worse than he thought. A lot worse. In fact, it needs to be completely replaced before there's any more damage to the structure underneath."

"O…kay…?'"

"Which means you'll need to find someplace else to live in the interim."

Her stomach dropped. "'Interim' meaning…?"

"Maybe…two weeks?"

"Oh."

Dazed, Jewel wandered out into the living room where her knees went kaflooey, sending her crashing onto the edge of the sofa. Doughboy, sensing unhappiness afoot, waddled over to nudge her thigh, offering slobbery condolences.

"It's really that bad?" she said.

"Worse. Noah said one good rainstorm and the whole east side of the roof could turn into a skylight."

Jewel doubled over, palming her face. "Where on earth am I supposed to go for two *weeks?*"

"You don't have friends or somebody you can stay with?"

Her face still buried in her hands, Jewel shook her head. And realized she was an inch away from acting like her mother. Hell. "I'll figure something out," she said, putting on her Brave Face as she stood, wiped her hands on her jeans and returned to the kitchen to check on the pork roast, which was dumb because the whole *point* of a slow cooker was not having to check on it—

"Um…"

She glanced up to see Silas doing that palming-the-back-of-his-head thing men did when they were dreading what came next. "If worse comes to worst, there's the sofa bed in the office."

"What office?"

"My office. Down the hall."

Clutching the cooker lid, she gawked at Silas. "You're asking me to stay here?"

"Only as an absolutely last resort."

She replaced the lid, muttering, "Your hospitality is overwhelming."

"You couldn't possibly *want* to bunk with me. Uh, us."

"After such a heartwarming invitation?" Jewel said, gathering placemats and flatware, then whooshing past Silas to set the table. "No. But like you said—" she smacked down the placemats, clunked the silverware on top "—I may not have a choice. And beggars can't be choosers and all that fun stuff."

"You're overreacting."

"You might not want to say that to a woman with a knife in her hand."

"It's a bread knife, I'll take my chances. And you just made my point—hey!"

Man was nimble, she had to give him that. Not that she'd

actually aimed the knife at him, it bounced off the floor a good foot from his shoe, but still close enough to make him jump. And, she was guessing by the dipped brows behind the glasses, seriously reconsider his offer. Pushing out a breath, she stomped over to snatch the knife off the floor and wash it, annoyed as all hell to feel tears coming on.

But, dammit, she was getting so tired of being in limbo, of not having her own home, her own life, of feeling torn in two between being there for assorted family members and desperately wanting, *needing,* to figure out who Jewel was—

"Jewel? The knife only fell on the floor, not into a pig sty. I think it's probably clean enough. And whatever's in the cooker smells fantastic, by the way."

She shoved down the faucet handle. Turned. Felt her renegade heart do a slow flip-flop at the contrite expression on Silas's face. Maybe his chivalry was a tad rusty, but this was a good man, as stalwart as they came. No, he clearly didn't want her there, but that didn't mean he didn't care.

"Sorry," she mumbled, swiping the knife through the dishtowel, then shoving her glasses back up her nose with the back of her hand. "You're right, I did overreact." One shoulder bumped. "But it's been one of those d-days—"

Oh, crud. There went her chin, going all wobbly on her. Jewel turned back to the sink, but it wasn't like she could hide wiping the tears. At least she wasn't all snotty or anything, but still.

"No, I'm sorry," Silas said softly. Gently. "I should've…" He sighed. "Ever since the boys' mother died—no, before that, when my marriage fell apart—I've had this problem with wanting to keep everything under control. Which is stupid because the more you try to make things go your way, the less inclined they are to do that."

"Tell me about it," Jewel said, folding her arms across

her ribs but still not looking at him. She sucked in a deep breath, then finally shifted her gaze to his. "I'm sure I can find someplace to stay, Silas. I mean, I appreciate the offer and all, but I'd never in a million years want you to feel uncomfortable. A night or two, that's one thing. But two weeks having a stranger in your house is asking a lot—"

The scream made them both jump. Like a flash, Silas was down the hall, Jewel right behind him, Doughboy lumbering along at the rear.

"I didn't do anything, I swear!" Ollie said, sobbing, rushing his father and clamping his leg. "Tad was just playing and all of a sudden he tripped and hit his head on the table, it wasn't even that hard, and then there was all this *blood!*"

Blood? That, she could handle. The look in Silas's eyes, not so much.

You'd think, with all the times Silas had seen, worn and wiped up his sons' blood over the last six years, he'd be inured to it by now. You'd be wrong. You'd also think a woman who got all emotional as easily as Jewel would fall apart at the amount of the red stuff oozing from Tad's forehead.

Wrong, again.

"Come here, baby," she said, calmly gathering the freaked, bloody little boy in her arms and steering him into the bathroom, where she hauled him up on the sink, grabbed a washcloth and carefully pressed it to the wound.

"I should be doing that," Silas belatedly called out over his other son's wails, which got him a "No, we're good, Ollie needs you," in reply.

"Blood doesn't bother you?"

"I'm studying to be a midwife, what do you think? Not to mention I was an ER nurse for six months…it's okay, sugar," she said to the other wailing child, "it's hardly more than a nick. Daddy? You got any butterfly bandages?"

"A lifetime supply. In the medicine cabinet."

"Is h-h-he okay?" Ollie managed between sobs.

"Oh, sure, baby—" She shot a smile in their direction. "There's just lots of blood vessels up there, so it looks a lot worse than it is. In fact, it's nearly stopped already."

As had the tears. From that corner, at least. Still. "Maybe we should take him to the ER, just to be sure," Silas said. "Head wounds are nothing to mess around with."

"True. But honestly, it's not that serious. Lord, if we'd trekked to the ER every time my stepbrother knocked himself in the head we'd've never left. Doesn't even look like it needs stitches. Come see for yourself."

Peeling his older son from his chest, Silas poked his head into the bathroom where Tad perched on the sink, swinging his legs and grinning. And true, the cut was so tiny you could barely see it between the scars from previous encounters with objects harder than his head.

"You feel dizzy?"

"Uh-uh," Tad said, shaking that head.

"Any trouble seeing?"

"I'm okay, swear. What's for dinner? I'm *starving*."

Smirking, Jewel slid her eyes to Silas's. "Do whatever you think best. But instead of sitting in the ER for three hours we may as well have dinner here and keep an eye on him. Or I can call Naomi, if you want…?"

Only doctor in probably three states who still did house calls. However… "No, that's okay. She…" He cleared his throat. "She's never actually said, but I can tell she thinks I—"

"Overreact?"

"You can stop smiling anytime."

She giggled. Only for some reason the sound didn't grate

nearly as much as Silas expected. Especially when she laid her hand on his arm and those soft, sweet eyes grazed his and she said, "At least your kids will always know you care."

And if that wasn't bad enough, then she got the boys—*his* boys—to eat pork that wasn't bacon. With *onions*. And *apricots*. Okay, so you could barely see the broccoli for the cheese sauce, but damned if that didn't disappear down their gullets—and not the dog's, Silas kept an eagle eye out to be sure—as well.

Of course, she did tell Ollie the planted broccoli spear in the rice was cute...but moments later, when a second spear appeared to keep the first one company, and Silas said, "Don't even think about it," and Ollie gave Silas his "testing" look and said, "Jewel thinks it's funny!" she immediately said, "What Daddy says goes, honey. Always."

"Then how come we got to play Secret City?" Tad piped up, and Ollie went, "Aww!" and Jewel flushed and said, "Pay no attention to him, that's the head wound talking," and Silas decided maybe losing some control wouldn't be such a bad thing.

Maybe.

Dinner over, the boys stampeded into the living room, Ollie grabbing the remote to find Nickelodeon, Tad flopping on the floor to use Doughboy as a pillow.

One eyebrow raised, Jewel turned to Silas. "You let them watch TV?"

"A half hour a day," Silas said, waving her aside when she tried to clear the table, wanting her gone. Wanting her to stay forever. Wanting to make an appointment to have his head examined.

Cocking hers, she listened for a moment, then snorted. "SpongeBob? Whoa. Subversive. Oh, shoot...where's my phone?"

Spotting the shimmying, hot pink, cutting-edge number on the counter, Silas felt the oddest sensation of…annoyance. Partly at the cutesy ringtone, but more because…because it was like being interrupted by an uninvited guest.

"Over here," he said, stacking the dishes by the sink.

"Thanks." Jewel zipped over and plucked off it the butcher block counter, said, "Uh-huh…uh-huh…be right there," then slipped it into a back pocket so tightly molded to her butt he had no earthly idea how she could fit a credit card in there, let alone a phone.

"It's Winnie Black," she said, her face all lit up, then vanished. For whatever reason, Silas followed her into the hall to watch her hustle to the front door to grab her purse and jacket. "Water broke, went right into hard labor—" struggling into the jacket, she yanked her ponytail out of the collar "—and it's her third birth, so I doubt it'll take too long."

"And you're telling me this why?"

Her hand already on the door knob, she gave him that What Planet Are You From? look. "Because I don't want you to worry about me getting here on time tomorrow? Hey, guys! I'm leaving! Come give me hugs!"

Didn't have to ask them twice. No small feat considering their undying devotion to all things SpongeBob. Both kids rushed over to nearly strangle her with hugs and kisses. For barely twenty seconds, mind, but the point was not lost on Silas.

Who, in the void left by her absence after her departure, found himself almost kinda wishing she'd given him one of those hugs, too.

Which point was not lost on him, either.

Chapter Five

*E*xhilarated.

That was the only word for it, Jewel thought as she and Patrice stood on the Blacks' front porch an hour after Jewel caught Winnie's seven-pounds-and-change baby girl. Behind them the wind sighed through the sixty-foot pine trees standing guard over the modern wood and glass structure tucked into the mountainside. And farther back, Aidan Black's studio where the Irishman captured, on enormous canvases, the majestic kaleidoscope of light and color that made up the landscape that Jewel, too, had grown to love so much.

"Couldn't've done it better myself," Patrice said, the yellow porch light skimming her high cheekbones and cropped silvery hair. Her broad grin. "Nobody could've told that was your first catch, missy. I'm proud of you."

Grinning herself, Jewel snuggled more tightly into her jacket and leaned against the porch railing. They'd go back inside shortly, but Patrice felt it was important to give the new family time to bond by themselves. "You might've given me warning, though, that you'd planned on turning over the reins."

"And have you fretting your head off beforehand? No damn way."

"I wouldn't have—" At Patrice's low chuckle, Jewel laughed, too. "Okay, I would've been a wreck, you're right. But what made you decide it was time I flew solo?"

"Couldn't really say. Same way I know when a baby's ready to come, I suppose. Even when the physical signs don't always agree with my intuition. You learn to feel these things, you know?"

Jewel released a breath. "Not like you do."

"Which is why you're the apprentice and I'm the boss," Patrice said, and Jewel smiled. "But I have no doubt whatsoever you will. I can tell already, could tell from the first time you attended a birth with me, you've got…I guess you could call it a gift, for listening and seeing with more than your eyes and ears."

Her face warming, Jewel looked away. "You're gonna give me a swelled head."

"You? Not a chance. So. How'd your first day go with the Garrett boys?"

"Fine," she said, her face heating even more at the memory of the conflicted looks Silas kept giving her. At the even more conflicted feelings those looks provoked inside her. Hormones Gone Wild were one thing; those, she understood. *Ka-BOOM,* however, was something else entirely. And far, far scarier.

Then she remembered a certain unresolved issue. "You know anyplace I can stay for a week or two?"

"Why? Eli throw you out?"

"No, no…the house needs some major repairs, that's all.

And the consensus is it'd be best if I vacate the premises 'til they're done. I don't suppose you and Lucy…?"

"Trust me, honey, you'd never get a wink of sleep on that sorry excuse for a couch. I slept out there when Lucy had that cold a couple of weeks ago and my back still hasn't forgiven me. I mean, if you can't find anything else, you're welcome to it. But I swear a bed of nails would be more comfortable."

"Believe it or not, it's tempting."

"And why is that?"

"Silas said I could have the pull-out in his office, but only if—" Jewel made quote signs in the air "—'worse came to worst'."

"And the subtext there is…?"

Speaking of hearing with more than her ears—nobody was better at that than Patrice. Even so, Jewel hesitated. Perhaps because her mother had always been the needy one, Jewel had long since learned to solve her own problems. That she even saw this as a "problem," however, was more of an eye-opener than she expected. That *Ka-BOOM* business and all. But maybe part of growing up was learning when to ask for help. Or at least, a fresh perspective.

"You ever find yourself attracted to somebody you know is no good for you?"

"Heh. Name me a human being who hasn't. Why? Oh… Silas?" When Jewel nodded, Patrice went, "I see. So what makes you think he's no good for you?"

"Oh, Lord…" Jewel leaned her elbows on the porch railing, only to smile when Winnie's border collie Annabelle nuzzled her hip for a scratch. "Where do I start?" she said, tangling her fingers in Annabelle's soft fur. "And anyway, it's more that we're not good for each other, if you know what I mean."

"Enlighten me."

Except when she opened her mouth…nothing.

"Yeah, that makes it clear," Patrice said, chuckling.

"Cut it out, I'm serious. Maybe I can't put it into words, but…but I know in my gut what I'm feeling…it's just not right. Dammit, Patty—I'm not like this! I don't hanker after things I can't have."

"And what makes you think you can't 'have' Silas?"

Jewel remembered how he'd looked at her over the dinner table, when he thought she didn't see, and thought, *Okay, maybe not the right word choice.* "It's no secret he's been resisting relationships since his divorce, so it's pretty obvious it really wrecked him. But it's been two years…" Her mouth pressed together, she wagged her head. "You ask me, all he's doing is hanging on to that safety net because it's what he's used to. Not what he really thinks anymore."

"Okay. And?"

"And…so…I think—even if he doesn't know it yet?— he's actually ready to take another shot. But no way is he gonna make the same mistake he did the first time around. Especially because of the boys."

"Makes sense. But I'm still not getting—"

"Only, see," Jewel said, straightening, "I sure as heck wouldn't be the right person for him, even if I was looking to get married—which I'm totally not because I'm trying to, you know, figure out who I am and all—because what the heck do I know about how to keep a marriage going? I mean, it's not like I've got any experience in that department!" She slapped her hand over her mouth, only to immediately lower it and whisper, "Did I really say that?"

"You really did." Smiling slightly, Patrice crossed her arms and leaned against the porch railing. "You do realize the only way to figure out how to make a relationship work is to just get in there and do it, right? Like catching babies—"

"And how many births did I have to observe before you felt I was ready to deliver a baby myself? And even so you were right there to cover my butt. Oh, Patty…it's not like I don't believe in good marriages—I see 'em, I know they exist. But not up close and personal. I have no earthly clue *how* those marriages work. How any marriage works. And I couldn't bear—"

"What?"

She looked at the other midwife. "I've seen way too many times the toll a failed relationship takes on all parties involved. I was only a baby when my father left, but twice after that I've helped my mother pick up the pieces, and each time she's more fragile than she was before. And to some extent I see the same hurt in Silas's eyes. That same 'why'? He probably doesn't even know it's there, but it is."

Patrice stared at her hard for a few seconds, then said, "Not that you don't have a valid point, but for heaven's sake, honey…talk about getting ahead of yourself. People get the hots for each other all the time. Doesn't mean they have to act on it. Or even if they do, doesn't mean it has to be more than what it is."

"And it's not like I don't know all that!"

"Then what's the problem?" A smile played around the older woman's mouth. "You think you're too weak to share quarters with the man without caving?"

Jewel forced a dry laugh. "Bingo?"

Patrice gave Jewel's arm a quick squeeze, then leaned back again, her hands shoved into her cargo pants' pockets. "Lord, you think things to death probably more than anybody I've ever met. But for what it's worth, I don't think you will."

"You don't think I will, what?"

"Cave."

"Really?"

"Not without giving yourself permission, no."

"You're not helping."

"That's 'cause you're a lot more fun to torment than my last apprentice. But I will say one thing—you want to shore yourself up so you don't cave, you might want to think about why you're looking into the man's eyes long enough to see whatever it is you think you see in there. Just a thought. Now," she said, pushing herself upright, "how's about we go check on mama and baby so we can maybe get home at a reasonably decent hour?"

Jewel managed to smooth out her crumpled forehead before going back into the Blacks' bedroom, where Winnie lay in the four-poster bed nursing her new baby girl, Aidan curled behind her. On the floor at the foot of their bed, their preteen son Robbie showed two-year-old Seamus how to run toy cars along the designs of the red, black and gray Navajo rug. For the first time that Jewel could remember since she'd started her apprenticeship, a weird, not-good, feeling shuddered through her, like when you think you might be getting sick but you're not sure.

She thought maybe it was called *doubt*. Not about her conviction that she wasn't meant to marry. God, no. But up until now she'd been perfectly at peace with that. Suddenly, though, something almost acidic seemed to nibble at the edges of that peace.

Something almost like...anger.

However, the minute Winnie looked up at her with her big, bright smile, the feeling passed, so quickly Jewel half thought she'd only imagined it. For her sanity, she was going with that. Because a momentary icky feeling about whether or not she was *happy*, for lack of a better word, didn't change anything, did it?

As for getting wigged out about the prospect of living in

Silas's house…that was just dumb. She *wasn't* her mother, she'd never in her life gone all weak in the knees over a man—heck, she'd never even gone through a boy-crazy stage when she'd hit puberty—so why on earth should she go down that road now?

*Ka-BOOM*S notwithstanding.

After arranging to check on Winnie and the baby the next day, Jewel said her goodnights and returned to her car, fully intending to take off right away. Instead, she sat behind the wheel for what seemed like forever, a soup of thoughts swirling in her brain, until one eventually bobbed to the surface: That her mother's emotions, her libido— heck, her very existence—had always seemed to be some- thing almost apart from her, acting completely on their own and leading their owner around by the nose.

Not Jewel, though. No way, no how. No, she couldn't control the outside stuff—like, say, leaking roofs—but she sure as heck could control how she reacted to them. How she reacted to, say, obviously lonely men with longing—and pain, no sirree, let's not forget the pain—in their eyes.

So. She could choose to be weak, or strong.

To be in control of her body, or let her body control her.

To sleep in her car for two weeks, or put her big girl pant- ies on and accept Silas's sofa bed offer. However grudgingly it had been given.

Right, then, she thought, finally backing out of the Blacks' driveway. *You can do this.*

Soon as she unearthed her copy of *Loin-Girding for Dummies.*

"So whaddya think about a Facebook page for the busi- ness?" Jesse, the "baby" Garrett brother said, half reclining in front of the office computer, his hands linked behind his shaved head. "It's free and takes like five minutes to set up. Couldn't hurt, right?"

Slipping into his jacket, Silas affectionately wondered, as he had many times before, how the multi-pierced, living graffiti display in front him had come from the same gene pool he did. But after a rocky few months a couple of years ago—during which Jesse had gotten his high school girlfriend pregnant, run off, returned and married her— the kid certainly appeared to have gotten his bald head on straight. He and Rach seemed to be doing okay, for one thing, and Jesse adored his baby girl. He'd also appointed himself the family's marketing director, and was apparently doing a bang-up job of it. Even their dad had to admit that if it hadn't been for Jesse's putting the business on the Web, the recession might have clobbered them a lot more than it had.

Silas smiled. "Couldn't hurt, I suppose. But ask the others, see what they think."

Nodding, Jesse hunched forward, his fingers flying over the keyboard. "So how's Jewel working out with the kids?"

Depends on who you ask, Silas thought, suddenly weary. And mildly anxious. Because if it was one thing he'd learned over the past week, when it came to Jewel, expecting the unexpected was the norm.

For her. Not him.

Whether it was having to peel sticky construction paper bits off the dog's feet—from a collage session with the boys that had reduced his kitchen to Lower Manhattan after the Yankees won the World Series—or hearing her shriek "Don't eat that!" a moment before the green "Jell-O" reached his mouth, or getting out of his car the precise moment a water balloon exploded in his face to say his nice, orderly world had been shattered would be a gross understatement.

However.

The boys were totally in love with her, for one thing. They were also both out like lights by 8:00 p.m. No hundred and one "I'm thirsties" or "I gotta pees" or not-so-stealthy belly crawls down the hall an hour after Silas thought/hoped/prayed they were asleep.

"Actually, it's working out okay," he said, even if he'd yet to sort out the weird combination of dread and anticipation that heralded his return home every evening.

"Cool," Jesse said, nodding. "So what's she gonna use the wood for?"

Silas froze. "Wood?"

"Yeah." More clicking, the intricate Native design on his brother's forearm gyrating in sync. "She came in earlier, asked Noah if we had any scraps."

Tap, tap, clickity-clickclickclick.

"And did he give them to her?"

"Huh? Oh. Yeah. Loaded a whole bunch in his truck and took it over there."

"When was this?"

"Dunno." *Clickity clickity click.* "A couple hours ago?"

Thinking *This can't be good,* Silas strode to his own vehicle, shaving a good two minutes off his previous shop-to-house record. The *wwwheeerrrrr* of a power saw, the *whack…whack…whackwhackwhack* of a hammer, his boys' war cries, reached from behind his house to slap him the moment he got out of his car.

He would've gone through the side yard but for the UPS package by his front door; grumbling, he snatched it up and went inside, tossing it on the coffee table as he passed hand-troweled plaster walls graffitied with taped-on leaves and the aforementioned construction paper projects. With great effort, Doughboy lifted his massive head from his customary nap spot in a pool of sunshine by the patio door. *Duuuude, make it stoooooop...*

"If only I could, boy," Silas muttered, yanking back the door to find his brother—shirtless, even though it stopped being warm ten degrees ago—sawing planks on a makeshift sawhorse while up in the tree Jewel was happily hammering away, singing at the top of her lungs.

"Hey, bro," Noah yelled over, shoving his safety glasses up on his sweaty forehead, a look only he could pull off and look good. Correction: Only he, Eli and Jesse could pull off and look good. "Whaddya think so far?"

"Of...?" Silas asked. Even though the hammering *in the tree* kinda gave him his first clue.

At that, Jewel popped up like the little Disney critter she was, all smiles and exuberant waves. From six feet over the ground. The hard, rocky ground that could easily break small limbs.

From the back of the yard the boys raced over, those small limbs churning and flapping like mad. "Uncle Noah an' Jewel are building us a *tree house!*" they both yelled at once, and Silas equally apportioned his glare between his brother and his new nanny.

"Boys, why don't you go inside and get Popsicles?"

"But we just had a snack," Tad said, even as, with a stage-whispered "Ssh!" Ollie yanked his baby brother across the yard and into the house.

Silence descended. As did Jewel, down the sturdy new ladder nailed into the mulberry's trunk. Thumbs hooked into her jeans' pockets underneath a neon pink hoodie, she walked over to Silas, Noah promptly joining her. "I thought you'd be pleased."

"Pleased?" he practically bellowed. "A tree house? For cripes' sake, Tad's only *four*—"

"But you said yourself—" ignore the tears, ignore the tears "—how great the mulberry was for a tree house!"

"When on *earth* did I say that?"

"The first day I sat for the kids! Remember? I mentioned how the tree was perfect, with those nice low branches, and you agreed!"

"I was making idle conversation, for crying out loud! Not putting in an order!" To avoid the imminent waterworks, Silas turned on Noah. "And how in the *hell* did you get dragged into this?"

"She asked me to help?" his brother said. "And what's with the wadded boxers, anyway? *We* had a tree house—"

"And both you and Eli broke your arms falling out of it!"

Scratching his head, Noah gave a sheepish grin. "We didn't so much *fall* as we sorta jumped. Although say one word to Dad and you're dead meat—"

"Not making me feel better."

"Bro. We were in middle school. And there were no safety rails. Not that that would've stopped us, probably—"

"I'm sorry," Jewel said in a small, defeated voice. "I thought…" She walked over to the picnic table and sank onto the bench, rubbing her arm. "I thought I was doing a good thing. Honestly. Especially when Noah got right on board—"

"There was your first mistake," Silas muttered.

"Hey!" Noah said, and Jewel almost smiled. Then she sighed.

"The boys are going to climb the tree, anyway, you know. At least now they'll have a good, solid way to get up there. And a safe, secure place to be once up. See?" she said, pointing. "Safety rails."

"And we could put barbed wire around the top so they

couldn't climb over," Noah said, backing up and laughing, his hands raised, at Silas's incredulous expression. "Just kidding, geez! Lighten up, man."

Lighten up? As if. However…air rushed from his lungs. The tree's very existence was an invitation to climb it. As well Silas knew, having climbed every vertical surface in the county when he was a boy. Not letting the guys have a tree house wasn't going to forestall the inevitable, Silas's druthers be damned.

The boys barreled back outside, wielding their frozen treats like swords as their high-pitched yells once more filled the air.

His heart.

"Is it finished yet?" Ollie screeched, bouncing around like a water drop on a hot griddle.

"Actually, honey…" Jewel started as Noah shot a hard look in Silas's direction.

"Actually, they were waiting for me to help," Silas said, rolling up his sleeves, and he thought Jewel's eyebrows were going to fly off her head.

Even though the temperature rapidly dipped once the sun set, it took more than a little nip in the air, Jewel discovered, to dissuade a Garrett brother from grilling outside. Odd, how barely two hours earlier she'd thought the brothers would come to blows—at least verbal ones—and now here they were, trading good-natured barbs as Silas grilled hamburgers and Noah gave him endless grief about his skills. Or lack thereof.

Then again, two hours ago she'd thought sure she was about to get canned. If not kicked out of the state.

Weird dude, that Silas.

Wrapped in a throw from the sofa with both boys huddled in their jackets next to her at the picnic table, Jewel watched Weird Dude, the softly flickering light from the grill caressing his sculpted features and making her tummy flop around like a fish out of water.

"Come and get it," he yelled, and the boys scrambled off the bench and over to their daddy. Naturally, they begged to eat up in their brand-new tree house, never mind that they had no idea how they'd get their food up there. Leave it to Uncle Noah, natch, to come up with A Plan; a minute later there was nothing but the sound of giggles and scuffling… and the occasional deep chuckle from their uncle.

Chuckling himself, Silas brought two plates over to the table, setting one in front of Jewel. "Cold?" he said in acknowledgment of her Indian Maiden getup.

"Freezing. You think we could move this inside? Noah's with them," she said when he glanced up at the tree. "They're perfectly safe."

"Like you said," he said with a half smile. "They're with Noah. Tell you what—how 'bout I start a fire in the pit on the other side of the patio? Will that do?"

When she nodded, he picked up both plates and headed across the yard, leaving her to shuffle along behind like a burrito with feet. A little later, seated on a cushioned patio chair and her limbs thawed, she finally found the guts to say what she hadn't before.

"I'm sorry. I really should have asked first. About the tree house."

Stretched out in a redwood chair a few feet away, Silas glanced over, took another bite of his burger. "Why? When you assumed you already had a go-ahead?"

She exhaled. "I might've…stretched that part a bit."

"Ya think?" At least she heard a smile in his voice. "Jewel," he said when she started to speak again, "I'm over it. Obviously. But, yes, you should have asked." His eyes grazed hers. "Don't assume. Please. Drives me bananas."

"Obviously," she echoed. "I won't do it again, I promise. Not consciously, anyway."

He laughed, the sound not as deep as his brother's but richer, somehow. More…sincere, she thought. Then he got up to stir the piñon logs in the pit, making sparks fly. From across the yard, the boys' laughter exploded from the tree the same way. Like sparks. Crouching in front of the pit, his back partially to her, Silas looked over for a moment then back at the fire.

"The sad thing is," he said, fiddling with the poker, "I probably would've built them the damn tree house myself. Eventually."

"Despite your mortal fear of broken limbs?"

Another soft laugh preceded, "Apart from locking the kids in a padded room for the rest of their lives, there's no way to prevent their getting hurt from time to time. Which I know," he sighed out, then stood, facing her. "It wasn't about keeping them safe as much as it was about keeping *me* safe. Or at least, me keeping control. You yanked the rug out from under me, Jewel, and I didn't take it well."

"I—I know. And I'm sorry—"

"Not your problem. And I mean that."

"Oh." She bit off another chunk of her burger, although her insides were shaking so much—and not only from the cold, despite the fire—she doubted she could get it down.

"So," he said, sitting again. "You find someplace to stay yet?"

He would bring that up. "'Fraid not."

"When you're ready to move in then, let me know."

Jewel stared at his profile for what seemed like forever before saying, very quietly, "You sure?"

"Not a bit."

She understood completely.

* * *

He could deal with the videos, as long as she didn't leave them out where the kids could load them and subsequently scar themselves for life. He could deal with the working model of a woman's innards, as long as she kept it in the closet in "her" room—again, due to the potential-scarring-for-life thing. Hell, he could even deal with the three boxes of stuffed toys which she'd insisted she couldn't leave behind in case, apparently, a typhoon struck while the roof was off and they got wet. Which, yes, required a Herculean effort on his part to swallow back a comment about grown women hauling around their Beanie Baby collection.

The books, however, nearly killed him. Literally.

"What the hell are these printed on?" Silas panted out, lugging in the deceptively small box. "Lead?"

"Wuss," Jewel said cheerfully, surveying the Beanie Baby-blitzed sofa. "And I saw that shudder."

"The boys don't have that many stuffed toys," he said, giving in to curiosity and prying out *Varney's Midwifery,* which was only marginally smaller than the base of his platform bed. "You've actually read this? Ow!"

She walked over to snatch the missile-ized puppy off the floor. "Open it."

He did. Highlighted passages everywhere. And scribbled, virtually illegible notes. "Huh."

"Yeah. Huh. I can't take my licensing test until I've got more hands-on experience, but you better believe they will not be able to catch me on any of the technical stuff."

Silas watched as she rammed a drawer overflowing with her unmentionables back into the small, beat-up chest they'd hauled over from Eli's house, still not fully at one with the idea of Jewel Jasper living in his house. She'd announced the morning after his offer that she was taking him up on it, right before she drove Ollie to school and without giving Silas a chance to back out. Which of course he wouldn't have, since it did appear he was her only option. But knowing it was only temporary? Not all that comforting, actually.

Hell, bad enough it took a good hour after she left the house for her scent to fade, for him to hug his boys and not smell her on their clothes. Now he was doomed to live in a Jewel-scented fog for a full week. Maybe two. As long as he was in the house, anyway.

Not that he would be all that much, what with her—and her herd of toys—taking over his office. Except at night.

Nights were going to be a problem—

"I'm guessing we'll have to share the bath?"

—as were mornings. Although she probably didn't have a whole lot of girl stuff to clutter the sink with. Didn't seem the type, somehow.

"Sure, no problem."

"Great!" She shoved Doughboy away from rooting around inside a tote bag large enough for Silas and his three brothers to sleep in, hefted it into her arms and lugged it out of the room.

Because he could, Silas followed her down the hall, standing at the bathroom door as he watched her unload the contents of the bag onto the sink. And the back of the toilet. And the rack in the tub. Which had previously held a single bottle of Head & Shoulders.

Yet another preconceived notion shot to hell. Although he now understood why she smelled so good.

"That's a lot of…stuff."

"Yeah, Mama feels duty bound to try every new product that comes on the market, only then she doesn't like nine-tenths of what she buys so she passes it on to me." She paused, carefully arranging a row of lotions on the back of the sink, then shrugged. "Every so often these random packages of jilted beauty aids arrive. Like Dillard's in a box."

"But you couldn't possibly use it all, either?"

Bright smile. "You'd be surprised. Of course, not all at the same time. But some days you want to smell like flowers, others like spice. Or almonds. You know how it is."

"Um, no, actually."

"Oh. I guess not, huh?" She giggled.

Gah.

Then her hands landed on her hips as she surveyed the array. "It really is a bit much, isn't it? You know what? Why don't I just take this…and this…and these—" she grabbed the tote, then plucked and scooped and snatched about half the bottles and jars into it "—back to the room, it's not like I need them *all*—"

"No, no…it's okay. You're a…guest."

She turned, all big of eye behind her glasses. "You're sure? I mean, I don't want you to feel like I'm taking over or anything—"

"Jewel. It's fine. Really."

A funny little smile flitted around her mouth before she ducked her head. "Well, okay," she said, slowly emptying the bag again. "If you're sure…" She held out one bottle. "Actually, you might like to try this yourself. It's this unisex stuff that works really great on dry skin. Lord, last winter my skin got so bad I thought I was gonna wake up one morning to find I'd shed it, like a snake."

Silas had to chuckle. "I know what you mean."

"Seriously, right?" she said, then motioned for him to step aside so she could return to the office.

Silas followed again, shoving his fingers in his pockets and leaning against the door jamb, watching her. Instead of, you know, going back to the living room or his room or the boys' room or anywhere where she wasn't. But no.

He nodded at the tiny tube TV on the floor next to the pelvis.

"I didn't think you could even find TVs like that any more."

"You can't. I've had this since I was six or something, my first stepfather gave it to me for my birthday. But, oh!" She turned. "Do you have satellite?"

"Yes, but—"

"Oh, good. Since it won't work without a dish or one of those converter boxes. Boy, are those things a pain."

"Jewel—we have a perfectly good flat screen in the living room which you're free to watch whenever you want."

"Thank you, but it's probably best if I stay in here, out of y'all's way, as much as possible. I've got a lot of studying to do anyway, so…" She shoved her hair behind a very cute ear. With three earrings. "And also, I sometimes like to watch TV real late, when I come back from a delivery? To unwind? I'll keep the sound down real low, I promise you'll never hear it. In fact, I may even have some earplugs around here somewhere—"

At this, she started riffling through an overflowing box she'd dumped on his desk. "Oh, good, here they are! Oh, no, those are to my MP3 player. Well, I'll find them, I'm sure—"

"Jewel!"

The earplugs dangling from her fingers, she looked up. "What?"

Man, was this gal doing a number on his head, or what? It was like there were two Jewels: the one who still kept stuffed toys and the one who'd studied and annotated a thousand-page textbook. The one who'd taken care of his bloodied child without so much as a flinch, and the skittish one who clearly felt like an interloper, even to the point of worrying that he might hear her TV at night.

At this point he couldn't even begin to pin down his reaction to her, a jumble of sympathy and annoyance, dizziness and—God help him—attraction. Which made no earthly sense whatsoever, what with him being all about sanity and control and her being all about plastic pelvises and water balloons and Beanie Babies.

And yet.

"Relax," Silas said, making himself smile. "You don't have to pretend you're not really here, okay? And if I gave you the impression you did..." He sucked in a breath. "I apologize."

For several seconds she treated him to one of those unreadable looks, then nodded. "Okay. Would you like...I mean, if you don't feel I'm overstepping things...would it be okay if I cooked dinner for you and the boys? I mean, regularly. When I'm not on a call, that is." She pressed a hand to her chest. "To say thanks for letting me stay here."

"You don't have to do that—"

"No, really—you'd be doing me a favor! I love to cook but there's not much point in going all out when it's just me. And it looks like you've got pots and pans you've never even used."

Silas waited for the pang to pass. "Then sure, knock yourself out. If that pork roast you made the other night is anything to go by, I'd be an idiot to say no."

Then she smiled, knocking the breath clean out of him, the void instantly replaced with the Not Good Feeling that'd taken nearly two years to finally fade, and he heard himself say in a voice probably rougher than it needed to be, "The pots and pans were Amy's. Stuff she bought right before things went south, so she wasn't doing much cooking after that. She took it all when we split, of course, but then..."

He rubbed a hand over his face. "I meant to sell it on

eBay or something, never got around to it. If there's anything you want, feel free to take it when you leave."

Then he walked away, counting his lucky stars the memories had smacked away the suggestion on the tip of his tongue, that if she was amenable, he wouldn't mind at all having someone to watch a grownup movie with, from time to time.

Dodged that bullet, boy. And thank God for it.

Chapter Six

"Who are these people again?"

Navigating the winding mountain road leading to the Blacks', Jewel smiled. Tad had asked the same question three times in the past hour.

"I told you, sugar—they're a family with a brand-new baby I helped bring into the world a week ago. And you're coming with me because your daddy has to work, and Mrs. Maple's got a doctor's appointment herself."

"Oh." Silence. "I'm glad. Mrs. Maple smells funny."

"Now, honey," Jewel said, practically biting her lip off so she wouldn't laugh, "that's not nice."

"S'true. And anyway it's not like I said it to her face or anything."

Poor Mrs. Maple. Their eighty-year-old neighbor was sweet as she could be, willing to take the boys *anytime,* it was no bother at all, she'd told Jewel. Except even Jewel had been nearly knocked over by the BENGAY fumes.

Even so, Jewel had been frankly surprised that Silas had so readily agreed to her taking Tad along. Well, after assuring him she didn't have so much as a parking ticket on her record, that Winnie was cool with her bringing an extra, and her swearing on her grandmother's grave there'd be no glimpses of anything untoward. Although Silas didn't know Jewel wasn't including breasts in that definition, since Winnie might want to feed her baby during the course of the visit—

Ohmigosh, her thoughts were jumping around like a bunch of fleas this morning. Probably on account of her not getting a lot of sleep last night, which she'd finally decided had a lot less to do with the lumpy sofa bed mattress than it did Silas going all weird on her when she'd mentioned the new pots and pans. Okay, *more* weird—the man was a species all his own, that was for sure. But for heaven's sake—how the heck was she supposed to know a few pieces of Paula Deen cookware would set him off?

Honestly.

And here she'd figured on the Beanie Babies doing that all by themselves. Not to mention all those bottles of girly-stuff in his bathroom—

"I gotta pee."

"We're almost there, sugar," Jewel said, turning onto the Blacks' private road. "Can you see the house?"

"Wow. It's all shiny."

What it was, was as sparkly as a big old diamond, the mid-morning sun flashing off all the glass walls and windows. Annabelle rushed them with barks of unbridled joy—*Company! This is the best day ever!*—sending the Blacks' housekeeper's small flock of chickens into a squawking frenzy.

Annabelle instantly commandeered Tad, much to his giggling delight, herding him over to Winnie's curious, thumb-sucking toddler, which in turn provoked a low laugh from the porch—Winnie herself, in slender jeans and a tailored shirt, not looking in the least like she'd given birth a week before.

"Looks like there's not much point in me being here," Jewel said as she climbed the dirt driveway toward the porch steps. The tall, easy-going blonde grinned.

"This one drains me dry in twenty minutes, then conks out for three hours. Unlike Seamus who was like a little barnacle for six months. Come on in," she said, holding open the beveled-glass front door as Jewel trooped up the steps. "Aisling's asleep in Daddy's arms."

"Tad, come on, sugar—"

"Oh, let 'em play. Annabelle won't let 'em out of her sight. Or the yard. Besides, we can keep an eye out ourselves from the living room window."

"You sure? 'Cause Silas…he worries."

"So I've heard. Although I don't suppose he's any worse than Aidan." She chuckled. "Some of us are just better at hiding it. Trust me—when you have kids, you'll understand."

Following Winnie inside, Jewel dumped her sweatercoat on the drum-like, pigskin *equipale* chair nearest the door. On the other side of the two-story room, Aidan sat staring at his brand-new baby girl, clearly awestruck. And sure, the look on his face made Jewel's insides go all mushy. Why wouldn't it? But every time people made comments like Winnie's, Jewel wondered…why? Survival of the species issues aside, why did people with kids assume reproducing was the only path to wholeness and fulfillment?

Obviously Jewel loved kids. And babies. And even teenagers—or at least one in particular. But for all sorts of reasons, it was by no means a given that she'd be a mama herself one day. So it kinda bugged her, the idea that her life would be crap unless she did.

Never mind the way her insides melted when she took little Aisling from her daddy's permanently paint-stained hands, inhaling her sweet infant scent as she carried her upstairs to her parents' cathedral-ceilinged bedroom. By this time, boys and pooch had come back inside; she could hear Seamus's high-pitched chattering as they both tromped up the stairs. Moments later the dark-haired toddler was by the bed, giving his new sister close to the same awestruck look as his father. Then he took her tiny hand in his not-much-bigger one and gave it an emphatic shake.

"How do, beebee?"

Seated on the edge of the bed, Winnie laughed. "Do you remember her name?"

The little boy's forehead puckered before he lifted wide blue eyes to his mother. "Aising?"

"Close enough," Winnie said, her wheat-colored hair sliding across her shoulders as she bent her head to her son's. Smiling, Jewel duly checked out the tiny, perfect girl, her big, slate blue eyes focused on Jewel's face as she kept up a soft conversation with the infant. In the midst of rediapering her, Jewel's phone rang.

"I'd better take this," she said, handing the gurgling infant back to her mother and walking out onto the open hall overlooking the light-flooded living room below. Amazingly, she hadn't heard from her mother in nearly a week, which gave her hope this wouldn't be one of "those" calls.

"Hey, Mama—what's up?"

"You busy, baby?"

"Out on an appointment, so I can't talk long—"

"Oh. Well. I'm headed up that way, sugar, so I thought

it might be fun to have lunch in Santa Fe, maybe take in a few galleries—"

"Mama?" Jewel said gently, never mind the not-so-tiny prickle of annoyance at the base of her skull. "Remember how I said I'm not free to go play whenever the mood strikes? Not that it doesn't sound like fun—" actually, the whole Santa Fe art scene was lost on her, but that was beside the point "—but I'm busy for the rest of the day. You go on ahead, though, enjoy yourself, okay?"

"I see," Mama said in her Hurt Voice. "You know, sometimes I get the distinct feeling you're trying to avoid me. I don't even have your real address! Just some silly old PO box number."

"I am not trying to avoid you," Jewel said, even though that's exactly what she was doing. "And everybody has a PO box up here, it's a real small town. But I really do need to go now. I'll talk to you later."

Maybe.

Soon after, her appointment finished and her charge gathered, Jewel headed back to town feeling far too unsettled for her liking—a feeling that only intensified as she drove past Eli's torn-up house, then on to Silas's, both places where she was only living temporarily, until—

Until when? Or, more to the point, until *what?*

Good question.

Yeah, apparently a nomadic childhood—as her mother got bored, got divorced, got remarried—combined with people moving in and out of her life like the tide had taken far more of a toll than she'd realized. No wonder she'd learned early on not to become attached to either person or place, because nothing lasted. Well, except her mother, who held the dubious distinction of being both the sole constant in Jewel's life as well as the cause of all that ebbing and flowing, she mused as she turned onto Silas's street.

Only to nearly have a heart attack when she saw Mama's Lexus coming down the street from the opposite direction.

Standing at the counter while he made himself a sandwich—Doughboy keeping a sharp lookout in case food met floor—Silas saw the sleek sedan glide up to the curb as Jewel pulled into the driveway. Saw, too, the trim, extremely attractive woman emerge from the gleaming, pearl-colored car and make her way on impossibly high-heeled boots toward Jewel, now out of her SUV and looking more miffed than he'd ever seen her.

He couldn't hear their conversation through the double-paned windows, but their body language spoke volumes—much wild gesticulating on the other woman's part, much head shaking and folded arms on Jewel's. Finally, tossing her hands in the air, Jewel went around to spring Tad; fingering his curls, she pointed toward the house.

Not that he expected to get much out of a four-year-old, but it was better than wandering into the fray himself.

"Who's that?" Silas asked mildly when Tad crashed through the front door.

"Jewel's mama. She's pretty. Whatcha eatin'?"

"Tuna sandwich. Want one?"

"Yeah. Please."

Silas grabbed a plate, keeping one eye on the scene outside his window. "Go wash your hands."

"They're not dirty," Tad said, shoving them close enough to get a good whiff of dog. "See?"

"Now, Tadpole."

With a dramatic sigh, the little boy trooped to the kitchen sink, climbing up on his Elmo footstool to wash. "Jewel said a bad word when she saw her mama's car. But real soft, so I don't think she knows I heard her." He banged down the faucet and jumped off the stool, knocking it over. "I think they're coming inside."

As indeed they were. Jewel entered first, her gaze reeking with apology, her mother following and talking nonstop—until she laid eyes on Silas, at which point her face lit up. "Oh, my," she said, gliding across the kitchen, her hand outstretched, her long, honey-colored hair billowing behind her. "And aren't you the handsome young man?" she said with an eerily familiar giggle. "I'm Kathryn, Jewel's mama. Silas, isn't it? It's *so* nice of you to take her in while her place is being fixed up."

Her place? Silas shot Jewel a look; she gave him a short, pleading headshake. As in, he was guessing Mama wasn't exactly up to speed on certain aspects of her daughter's situation.

Since no way in hell was he getting anywhere near that one, Silas turned back to Kathryn, her expertly applied makeup emphasizing high cheekbones and deep-set gray eyes underneath windblown bangs. "Only glad I could help," he said, earning him another, more flirtatious giggle. She had to be in her forties, at least, but she barely seemed older than her daughter. Not only because of the way she was dressed—jeans a little too tight, the frilly blouse's neckline a little too low—but because of the hyper vibes she gave off.

Fingers tipped with fake, square-edged nails briefly touched Silas's arm as Kathryn lowered her voice. "For the life of me I cannot understand why on earth she wants to be a *midwife*. I keep telling her—what man's gonna want to marry somebody who leaves the house at all hours to go deliver babies?"

When Kathryn turned to Jewel—oh, did she remember her daughter was standing right there?—Silas looked over, embarrassed as hell for her. But Jewel stood with her thumbs hooked in her jeans' belt loops, a slight smile curving her lips as though her mother's words had no power whatsoever to hurt her. Even if the cherry-red blotches on her cheeks gave the lie to that little subterfuge.

"Although," Kathryn went on, oblivious, "I don't know why I worry, I imagine you'll get over it soon enough. Just like when you did that play in high school, and decided you wanted to be an actress. Or that band you were in for, what? A month? One thing about you, you never stuck with any of your crazy ideas long enough for me to get overly concerned. By the way—I ran into Justin the other day, did I tell you? I'd bet you anything you could get him back like that," she said, snapping her fingers. Then, to Silas, "She was engaged to this absolutely *lovely* young man, his daddy owns one of the biggest ski resorts in Taos, she would've been set for *life*. But was that good enough for her? No."

"Mama?" Jewel said softly, the slight shake in her voice making Silas's skin prickle. "Not the time or place—"

"Well, when *is* the time, since I can't even remember when we last spent five minutes together? My goodness, I've never even seen where you live!" Kathryn's attention immediately flitted away, her fingers constantly toying with the delicate gold chain at her neck as she clicked across the tiled floor to peer into the great room. "My goodness, isn't this just the *sweetest* place! I just love these old adobes, they've got such a sense of *history,* don't you think? Did your wife do the decorating?" She turned, giving Silas a quick head-to-toe. "Or…did you?"

Hotheaded, Silas was not. In fact, when taunted as a kid he'd been far more inclined to either walk away or stare the tormentor down rather than get physical. Yet here was this scrap of a woman getting under his skin so bad it was everything he could do not to bodily remove her from his house. "I'm not married, Mrs. Jasper—"

"Oh, honey, I haven't been Mrs. Jasper in more than twenty years. I'm back to my maiden name now—DuBois—it's just easier that way. And it's okay, honey, I *understand*." This said with a wink.

"For heaven's sake, Mama—!"

"I'm a widower, Ms. DuBois. Although we were already divorced. So I'm never sure which it is, actually."

"That must be *so* hard on your little boy," Jewel's mother said with a smile for Tad, who'd come back into the kitchen and seemed understandably leery about taking his seat at the table. Like a moth with ADD, Kathryn was in constant motion, her nearly incessant speech frequently punctuated with that nervous, high-pitched giggle. Which Silas now realized was *nothing* like Jewel's.

"I know it was rough on Jewel, after her daddy left. Which was why I remarried, so the poor baby would have a daddy. Only that didn't work out, unfortunately. So I tried again, and that didn't work, either—I suppose she's told you all about that, though. No—?"

"Okay, Mama," Jewel said, holding out one arm in an attempt to guide Kathryn outside, "Silas needs to get back to work, and so do I—"

"I'm sorry, am I interrupting—?"

"Yes, actually. Besides if you don't get a move on you'll barely have time to do Canyon Road before it gets dark. And you know how you hate driving at night."

"Oh! I thought I could stay with you tonight—"

"And as you can see that's not an option," Jewel said, her firmness a little tentative, like the first few minutes behind the wheel of somebody else's car. "Come on, I'll walk you out."

Silas watched through the kitchen window as, to his shock, Jewel embraced the woman—as opposed to shoving her behind the wheel and slamming shut the door, which would have been his inclination—then stood with her arms crossed as Kathryn drove off.

And he thought his relationship with *his* mother was complicated.

His sandwich finished, Tad hauled a reluctant Doughboy out back to play, the patio door banging shut right before Jewel returned to collapse at the table, her head in her hands. "I can't imagine what you must be thinking right now." Her head lifted. "I have no earthly idea how she even found me."

"She really didn't know where you were living?"

"Oh, she knows I'm in Tierra Rosa, but…no." She lifted her head, her lips pressed together. "I tried to stop her, but it's like trying to hold back a tsunami."

Silas smiled. "Sort of like my mother?"

"Oh, Lord, no. Donna's one of the strongest, most capable women I've ever met. Mine…isn't. Not emotionally, anyway."

"She's certainly capable of mortifying her daughter in public."

Jewel almost laughed. "Her way of showing she cares."

"And it doesn't bother you?"

Her gaze lifted to his, eerily calm, like the slate blue sky right before a whopper storm. The corners of her mouth tilted in a humorless smile. "Are you kidding? My scars have scars. I mean, who doesn't try on a dozen different personalities in high school, seeing what fits and what doesn't? But…"

She sighed. "I was a straight A student, Silas. I worked my butt off in nursing school, graduating near the top of my class. Mama's not stupid, but she barely made it through high school, never went to college. Lord knows I've got issues about…other things, but I'm good at what I do. And

I know it. When she gets going like that, I can never quite tell if she's truly worried that I'll fail—by her definition, anyway—or it simply hurts her too much to acknowledge I'm successful in ways she never was."

Good Lord. If Amy's mother had done that to her, his ex would have bitched and moaned for a week. That Jewel seemed so philosophical about the whole thing was blowing his mind. And almost pissing him off. "Then why on earth do you let her get away with that crap?"

"Because I can?" Jewel said dryly. "Hey, there's a reason she only knows my PO box. And why I said we don't talk all that much. She would suck me dry, if I let her." She blew a short laugh through her nose. "Neediness and disapproval are a killer combination."

"Hence your not wanting her to know you're going through a rough patch."

"And give her ammunition? Oh, *heck,* no. But Mama can't help who she is. *What* she is. So I stick close enough to pick up the pieces when needed, but far enough away to preserve my sanity." She started to rise. "And I'm sure you've got better things to do than listen to me yammer about my mother—"

"Next appointment's not until two." The dog scratched at the door, begging to be let back in. Silas obliged, then said, "In fact…how about a sandwich?"

He could sense her waffling. "You don't have to—"

"Done," he said, placing the sandwich in front of her. "Tuna and mayo on white bread. Even I can't screw that up."

Granted, being dragged into somebody else's family dynamics was the last thing Silas needed. Or wanted. Nor was he clear about his motives for sticking around—morbid curiosity? That protectiveness thing again? Who knew? Whatever it was, he scraped back a chair and sat across from this intriguing young woman who clearly loved her screwed-up mother, only to suppress something approaching a shudder when her eyes grazed his, a sad smile pulling at her mouth.

"Once I get going I'm not sure I'll be able to stop."

"I'll take my chances," Silas said, surprised to discover he honest-to-God meant it.

For some reason Jewel never talked about Mama to anybody. Not her college roommates, not even Patrice. She wasn't sure why. Which made her wonder even more why spilling her guts to Silas seemed perfectly normal. But she felt like there was all this stuff boiling up inside her, that if she didn't let it out it would burn her alive. And also, like maybe if she gave voice to all these tangled-up thoughts, somehow they'd get untangled and start to make sense.

At least, talking couldn't make things any worse, right?

After toying with her sandwich for several seconds she finally tore off a corner, gesturing with it and giving poor Doughboy false hope. "Mama was a figure skater. When she was a kid, I mean. I've seen tapes. She was good. Real good. Good enough that there was apparently talk of her being Olympic material. Except the year she had her first real shot at Nationals, she went boy crazy and lost her focus. Both her grades and her skating went south."

Silas propped his cheek in his palm. "How do you know this?"

"My grandmother—her mother—told me, shortly before she died, when I was ten. Anyway, by the time Mama graduated from high school—by the skin of her teeth, she was not one of those overachievers who could practice four hours a day and still keep a 4.0 average—her shot at Olympic glory was long gone, but she was still good enough to join one of those ice shows."

The first bite of sandwich stuffed into her mouth, she tore off another and fed it to the dog. Made the beast's day. "Six months later, she was married to one of the guys in the tour and pregnant with me."

"Ouch."

"Yeah. One of those life-altering moments. From which she never fully recovered, if you ask me. Or moved past. Her skating career was in the toilet, she had a subpar education, a kid to raise and insufficient ambition to overcome any of it. All she had was her looks. And yes, she's still gorgeous, you can say it."

"If you like that type."

"She's a stunner, Silas. Something I wouldn't be if every makeup salesgirl at Macy's had at me for a week," she said with a rueful laugh, ignoring Silas's pole-axed expression to add, "And what Mama mostly stuns, is men. Except, unfortunately, once the jolt wears off they all fly away." She made a little flapping motion with her fingers. "Including my father, when I was two. Although that's at least kinda understandable, what with my being the product of an ice-show fling and all. It was the two daddies after that…sorry. If I start to sound bitter, stop me, 'kay?"

Silas had sunk back in his chair by now, one wrist on the table, his other hand stroking Doughboy's head. "You don't think you're allowed to feel bitter?"

"I'm allowed, sure. If I want to go down that road. I don't. I want to find a way out of the muck, not wallow in it. And to that end, I finally figured out that Mama keeps picking men whose maturity level matches hers. Which makes them fun as all heck to be around, but eventually both parties get bored, like a pair of four-year-olds who don't want to play anymore. So the men left. Over and over and over, they left."

She shrugged, an old, ingrained habit. One Silas apparently saw straight through when he gently said, "Except… it wasn't only your mother they were leaving. Was it?"

Her stomach heaved as she suddenly saw the double line in the sand. One was hers, gouged years before, the other Silas's. Not that she'd cross, but holy-heck-on-a-stick if she hadn't crept close enough to send a grain or two tumbling into the insubstantial crevice. On her side, at least.

Her lips parted a moment before she grabbed her plate and glass and bolted to the dishwasher, at which point she realized Silas had already crossed both lines and was on her side and what did she intend to do about that?

"Sorry—"

"No, it's okay," she muttered, putting her dishes into the washer and pushing shut the door. Then she turned, her arms tightly folded over her quaking middle as she amassed the necessary forces to shove him back across before there was more than *sand* finding its way into crevices. "God knows I had no intention of going down this road today, but since I'm taking care of your kids—and since you've met my mother—you should probably know what my Looney Tunes potential is."

"And there you go overreacting again. I don't think—"

"So, yeah," Jewel said, ignoring him, "by the time Aaron's father bid us *adios* I realized you can only watch so many people walk out of your life before you shut down, at least to some degree. It wasn't something I consciously did, I don't think…but whatever it is that makes people take that chance on another person? It wore out a long time ago. Meaning I'm apparently as relationship impaired as my mother is."

Silas's brows crashed together. "A conclusion you've

reached at twenty-five?" At her raised brows, he mumbled, "Sorry, that was out of line—"

"No, actually, it's a valid point. Especially since…"

She reached up to fiddle with her ponytail while she chose her words.

"It's kinda hard to grow up yourself when you don't exactly have the best example in the world. You saw Mama—does that look like somebody who subscribes to *US News & World Report?* So I'm kinda way behind the curve, here. Maybe I've made enough progress to know all my screws aren't as tight as they should be, but I've got a long way to go before I can be taken out in public. If that day ever comes."

Silas's brows crashed together. "Why are you being so rough on yourself?"

"I prefer to think of it as b-being realistic," Jewel somehow got out over the tremors racking her body from the bizarre combination of compassion and irritation in his eyes. She swallowed, steadying herself. "I know you think I act like a kid sometimes—no, don't try to deny it, your face is like a giant billboard. But if I do, that's because I still feel like one in a lot of ways. Doesn't mean I'd ever put your kids in danger, but it does mean that…that maybe I relate more to them than I do to a lot of so-called adults."

His eyes never leaving hers, Silas quietly said, "You relate to this adult just fine," which got the tremors going all over again, threatening to rattle her brain loose from her skull, and she thought, *O-kay, chickie, time to change the subject.*

Which she did by saying, "Hey…I noticed this morning you're out of, gosh, practically everything. Why don't I take Tad to the store and do some stocking up? I make fried chicken that'll make you weep, no lie."

* * *

Their gazes held for several seconds, hers clearly pleading to let the conversation—and her—go.

"That sounds great," Silas said at last, realizing if you open the can of worms you've got no right to get upset if they crawl away. Or all over you.

"Okay, then," Jewel said, swinging her arms and backing toward the doorway leading to the hall. "I'll see you later, then. Um, thanks for lunch." *Because this conversation? It never happened.* "Tad! Wanna go to the store, baby?"

A few minutes later Silas stood at the kitchen window watching a giggling Jewel strap his little boy into his booster seat, then carefully back out of the driveway and slowly drive off, and his things-are-supposed-to-add-up brain registered that…things didn't. At all. That her words and her body language, what she said and what she *did,* were at complete odds with each other.

And that his pitiful left-brained soul wouldn't rest until he figured it—her—out.

Chapter Seven

"C'n we go see Gramma before we go home?" Tad asked as they loaded the groceries into the car. Well, Jewel loaded, Tad was doing the ants-in-the-pants wiggle. Jewel, however, being the designated adult—hah!—had to confine her wiggling to the unseen variety, never mind that she was about to pop right out of her skin. Holy moley.

"Can't, sugar, I need to pick your brother up from school—"

"But it's on the way! And I miss Gram-*ma*—" he launched himself at the tailgate, bounced off, did it again "—'cause we haven't seen her in for-*ev*-er."

Moving the child aside to slam shut the hatch, Jewel sighed, then finger combed those irresistible curls. "I know, sugar, but the school's actually in the opposite direction. And we've got perishables in the car."

"What's that?"

How I feel when your father looks at me.

"Stuff that'll go bad if it's not kept cold." She opened the back door and pointed. "In."

Scowling—and looking so much like his father Jewel nearly choked on a laugh—Tad crossed his arms over his chest. "I'm not a baby—why can't I sit in front with you?"

"Does your father let you do that?" He slid a "You're kidding, right?" look to her and she smothered another laugh. "Uh-huh. So don't even go there, buddy. The law says little dudes have to sit in the back in a booster seat because that's where it's safest. So come on, or we're gonna be late picking up Ollie."

"Life is so not fair," the kid grumbled as he climbed into the seat and let her buckle him in.

"Too true, sweet pea. But…why don't I see if your Gramma and Papa can come over for dinner? Seeing as I bought enough chicken to feed half the town, anyway."

Not to mention having other people around would distract her from Silas's too-knowing looks. His too-kind eyes. Because it would not do to succumb to those eyes, to let herself even get near the same trap that'd taken far too many chunks out of her heart already. Not to mention her hide.

"Yeah! C'n I call 'em? I know the number."

Of course he did. Jewel dug her cell phone from her purse and handed it to the four-year-old, who studied it for maybe two seconds before punching in the number. "C'n you get on the Internet and stuff with this?"

May as well fill out his MIT application now and be done with it. "So they say. My mama gave it to me a couple of months ago, but I haven't had a chance to really play with it." Meaning she was too much of a techno-boob to figure half of it out. Long as she could make and receive calls and text, she was good.

"Gramma says they'd love to come," Tad said a minute

later, holding the phone to his chest. "What time and can she bring anything?"

"Tell her six, and no. I've got it covered." A little fizz of excitement tickled the pit of her stomach, bubbling away at least some of the anxiety from that little tête-à-tête with Silas earlier. It'd been ages since she'd cooked a big meal. If she hurried, she could even make a cake….

"Gramma says to tell you you're an angel," Tad said, handing her back the phone and looking hugely pleased with himself. Warmth suffused Jewel as she leaned over to tickle Tad's sweatshirted tummy—man, those things were like magnets, weren't they?—then walked around to get in behind the wheel, wondering why the more she tried to wrest control out of the chaos that was her life, the more complicated it got.

Honestly.

The intoxicating scent of baking chocolate, the squeals of laughter and low-pitched barks, all punched Silas in the gut the instant he walked inside. He paused, frowning, until something thumped him on the back of his head and said, *It's called happiness, idiot. Remember?*

Pocketing his keys, he headed—with some trepidation—toward the source of the noise and the aroma to find his two mini-mes and their sitter chasing each other around the kitchen armed with mixer beaters and wooden spoons… flinging some sort of gooey substance at each other. Hence the dog's frenzied barking, interrupted every couple of seconds or so to schlurp frosting blobs off the floor. The cabinets. A child.

He'd forgotten how messy happiness often was.

"Daddy!" Ollie shrieked, zooming over to share the joy. And, no doubt, the aforementioned gooey substance.

"Gramma and Papa are comin' to dinner, an' Jewel made a cake, and we helped! It's gonna be de-*lic*-ious!"

Silence descended, except for the rhythmic schlurp, schlurp, schlurp of Doughboy's washcloth-sized tongue against the far wall.

"Oh, um…hi?" Jewel said, panting and clearly trying to squelch the laughter. A huge, cream-colored smear completely obliterated one side of her glasses. She cleared her throat, then removed her glasses to wipe the dirty lens on her shirttail. "Didn't expect you home so soon."

"No kidding."

They locked gazes for a moment before she said, "Guys? Go get cleaned up and change. Toss your clothes in the laundry, I'll wash them while I'm doing the rest of dinner."

The boys dashed off, bumping into and shoving each other—

"And don't touch anything before you get those clothes off and your hands clean!" Jewel yelled after them, then turned back to the mixer bowl on the island, wiping her hands on the seat of her pants. Beside the bowl sat three dark chocolate cake layers, cooling on wire racks. "Honest to God, I have no idea how that happened. One minute Ollie was helping me stir the frosting, and the next thing I knew all heck broke loose."

"I take it you're feeling better?"

Her eyes zinged to his, then skittered away. "I have no idea what you're talking about."

"Jewel—"

"Hey, Doughboy—how ya doing over there?"

The beast glanced over, butt wriggling and jowls jiggling, then returned to his chore, happy as a pig in slop. Or a bulldog in a frosting-splattered kitchen. Clearly unfazed, Jewel dunked a wooden spoon into the big metal bowl on the counter, then held it out to Silas. "Buttercream frosting.

Been wanting to make it forever but never had a reason. Go on, taste. It's a clean spoon, no cooties."

She had frosting in her hair. Her cheek. Over her left breast.

Silas hesitated, then tasted.

"So...?"

"It's...okay."

Jewel laid the spoon across the bowl and folded her arms, which is when she noticed the blob on her boob. She scooped it off with her index finger, stuck her finger in her mouth. "You mad because we made a mess, or mad because you weren't part of the fun?"

"I'm not mad..."

Are, too.

Fine, so he was mad. But not about the mess. No, he was mad about how this gal was getting to him, about how she could make the boys laugh like that when he couldn't, about how he'd sworn to steer clear of women with issues he had no clue how to handle and here this one lands right in his lap, boom, about a thousand other things he couldn't even pin down long enough to name.

But mostly he was mad about feeling like he was being stretched in a dozen different directions, about finding himself in this strange new place where he felt so out of control—of his kids, his home...his feelings.

And it was all Jewel's fault. Except it wasn't.

"I'm not mad," Silas repeated, reaching for the spoon and another bite of frosting. "Confused, maybe, but not mad."

After a loooooong silence, she muttered something that sounded like "Welcome to my world."

"Except about this," Silas said, jabbing the spoon at the frosting. "*This* is quite possibly the best damn thing I've ever tasted in my life."

Doughboy woofed in agreement and went back to licking. The front of the stove, this time. Jewel laughed, then turned a bright smile on Silas that only made him more confused.

Especially when it vanished as abruptly as it had appeared.

"I have to say, Jewel," Silas's father said, his hands cradling a belly well-rounded *before* he'd consumed four pieces of fried chicken and made-from-scratch chocolate cake with buttercream frosting, "you're *almost* as good a cook as my Donna." This, Silas noted, with a wink for his mother, who, knuckling her cheek, gave his dad a sly smile followed by a gentle slap on his forearm.

"And I will consider that high praise indeed," Jewel said with a smile as she stood to gather the dishes off the kitchen table, only to give Silas a funny look when he practically snatched the nearly empty chicken platter out of her hands.

"You cooked, the boys and I will do the dishes. Won't we, guys?" he said pointedly to his progeny, who reluctantly slid from their seats and trudged over to the trash to begin scraping the bone-heaped plates already on the counter. No fool he, Doughboy roused himself from his bed by the back door and lumbered over to keep them company.

Donna laughed. "Your poor daddy's about had it with heated up casseroles from the church ladies. And *where* did you learn to bake like that?"

Although Jewel had relinquished the clean-up duty easily enough, now she stood by the counter with her hands stuffed in the pockets of her lightweight sweater, as if she wasn't sure what to do next.

"When I was a little girl, we lived next door for a while to this lady who won all sorts of awards and stuff for her cakes and pies. One day I asked her if she'd teach me, and she said okay. That was her fried chicken, too." She sort of laughed. "Mama was never much of a cook, so I learned how in self-defense."

Silas glanced over in time to see her flush, shove a piece of loose hair behind her ear. "Um...if you don't mind, I'd like to get some studying done tonight. Unless you want me to help with the boys...?"

"No, you go on," Silas said. "Technically you're off duty at five, anyway."

Then, because clearly his brain had taken off for parts unknown, he stared after her as she left.

A minute or so later, their chore done, the boys grabbed their Papa's hands and dragged him into the living room to read to them. Leaving Silas alone with his mother.

"That gal's the sweetest thing, isn't she?"

Silas rinsed the platter and stuck it in the dishwasher. "I suppose."

"Real fine cook, too. And the boys certainly seem fond of her—"

"Ma. Don't."

Instead of taking offense, Donna patted the chair beside her. "Quit that for a minute and come sit."

Expelling a huge breath, Silas scrubbed his hands on a dishtowel, lobbing it at the counter before he slumped into his chair like a pissed-off teenager. His mother chuckled, a halo of rebellious hair floating around her nearly wrinkle-free face. "It must really suck, having such a bully for a mama."

"Like you wouldn't believe," he said, his mouth pulling into a smile despite himself.

Donna laughed again, then propped her chin in her hand, the twinkle fading from her eyes. "That gal's a real lost soul, isn't she?"

Silas's eyes narrowed. "Don't think she's interested in being saved, Mom."

His mother's chest wobbled when she chuckled. "The ones who most need it usually aren't. But I'm not talking about matters of faith, I'm talking about that look in her eyes, like she's scared at any moment she's gonna get the boot. And out of all my boys," Donna continued with a tender smile, "you were the one most likely to bring home baby birds and the like. Unfortunately for you, that baby bird's got a broken wing you haven't yet figured out how to fix."

Not looking at his mother, Silas tapped his thumb against the table for several seconds before saying, "Let's just say stability wasn't exactly a hallmark of her childhood." At his mother's raised brows, he said, "Her mother showed up out of the blue earlier today," then shared the more salient points of the conversation that had followed.

"I see."

"Good for you, 'cause I sure as hell don't."

"Guess that depends what you're looking for."

"I'm not *looking* for anything."

"Don't be silly, of course you are. We all are. Even if we don't know it. And yes, I'm going all flower child on you. Deal with it. Look," she said, leaning closer, "something about Jewel's obviously troubling you. Or at least perplexing you. No shame in that." She smiled. "And I promise I won't read more into it than there is."

"That'll be the day," Silas said, and his mother lightly smacked his shoulder. Then he sighed. "It's her whole 'I'm just a kid' schtick—I'm not buying it."

Using a discarded napkin to sweep up crumbs from the table, Donna said, "Noah said the same thing, not two days ago."

Silas frowned. "Noah?"

"What, he's not allowed to have an opinion?"

"Of course he is, but…"

"But…?" Donna coaxed, her mouth twitching.

"Nothing," Silas irritably mumbled, crossing his arms. "What, exactly, did he say?"

"Same as you, more or less. That her ditzy routine's an act. He saw through her in a heartbeat. But then, I suppose Noah has more experience with that sort of thing than you do."

"And you say that like it doesn't even bother you."

"Oh, Noah will find his way. Or rather some woman will find him, and the poor boy won't know what hit him. But that's a crisis for another day. Right now we're talking about Jewel. And her mama." Donna's brow bunched. "A figure skater, huh? To get as far as she did—that takes a lot of discipline."

"And what does that have to do with anything?"

"I'm not sure. But you know me, looking for the good in everybody."

One side of Silas's mouth hiked up. "Even Jewel won't come right out and accuse her mother of messing her up. According to her, Kathryn's not a bad person, just clueless—"

The doorbell rang.

"Got it!" Jewel yelled as she sprinted from her room, phone in hand, to yank open the door and let out a strangled shriek; Silas arrived on the scene just in time to witness her hauling some skinny, shaggy, baggy kid into her arms.

Only to let go, slug him in the arm, yell, "What the heck were you *thinking?*" then hug him all over again, until the grinning kid untangled himself from her grip enough to look up and say, "Oh, hey—you must be Silas, huh?"

"Uh, yeah. And you are?"

The grin stretched so far the boy's ears rose a half inch.

"Aaron. Jewel's stepbrother."

"I cannot *believe* you hitched!" Jewel said, slapping her brother on the arm through his thick hoodie before setting a plate piled with fried chicken and mashed potatoes and gravy and coleslaw in front of him. The first but probably not the last, she was guessing, since he'd already edged past six feet at *fifteen,* for God's sake. Silas's parents had gone back home, although Donna gave her the requisite "Let us know if you need anything" spiel before she left, and Silas was putting the boys to bed. Leaving Jewel mercifully alone with her brother so she could smack him around without witnesses. "Are you *insane?* You want tea or milk?"

"Milk, please. And I didn't exactly hitch—" Aaron grabbed the glass from her before it reached the table, gulped half of it down "—I got a ride from my friend's older brother's best bud, he was coming down to Albuquerque, anyway."

"Then why didn't you say that to begin with?" Jewel said, dropping into the seat catty-corner to him, watching him stuff food in his mouth like he hadn't eaten in weeks. "You said 'hitched'—" Then she shook her hands. "Never mind. But how did you find me here?"

"You said it was a small town, everybody knew everybody else's business—I asked at that Mexican restaurant, the lady at the register told me where you were."

Probably how her mother had found her, too. Which was neither here nor there. She frowned. "And…how did you get from there to here?"

"Some dude at the restaurant brought me. It's okay, the

same lady said I'd be fine, and she doesn't look like somebody you'd mess with."

"Big gal? Older? Dyed black hair?"

"Yeah."

"That's Evangelista, she owns the place. And you're
right, nobody'd mess with her. But, Aaron, honey…" She
dipped her head to look up underneath his straggly, dish-
water blond bangs. "You can't stay here. You've gotta go
back and work this out with your dad."

"No way, sorry." His head wagging, Aaron stripped half
the meat off a drumstick with one bite. "He's getting *married* to that chick I told you about. Witch Woman." He
barely glanced at Jewel, but long enough for her to catch
the tears. Damn.

"Oh, sweetie…" Sighing, she sagged back in the chair,
her arms crossed. "I hurt for you, I really do. But this isn't
even my house, there's barely room for me in the office,
let alone you—"

"I don't mind, I've got my sleeping bag. You won't even
know I'm here, promise. Besides, you said your place will
be fixed in a week or so, right?"

"That's not my house, either." When Aaron frowned
at her, chewing, she waved her hand again. "Never mind.
Aaron. You're not listening—"

"I thought you missed me?"

"Of course I miss you! Like you wouldn't believe! But…I
can't take care of you—"

"And like I said, you don't have to *take care* of me. I'm
not helpless! I just…need someplace to stay."

"Oh, geez, baby—"

"It's totally okay with Dad. And for cripes' sake, I'm
not a baby!"

No, he definitely was not. Except for the zits peeking
through the bangs and the peach-fuzzed lip and teary

eyes. Jewel sighed. "So if I called him right now, he'd say that."

The kid's honey-colored eyes meeting hers, he dug out his cell phone and handed it to her. "Go ahead—" Then looking past her, he stood so fast his chair tipped backwards. "I didn't mean to be any trouble, Mr. Garrett," he said, fumbling for the chair before it hit the floor, his cheeks bright red when he shoved his hair off his forehead. "I honestly had no idea Jewel wasn't in her own place, sir. I'm sorry."

Silas stared hard at her brother for several seconds, then rammed his hands into his back pockets. "And maybe," he said quietly, "you should've found out exactly what your sister's situation was before simply showing up and upsetting her."

Jewel's mouth fell open. "I'm not—"

"Yeah, you are," Aaron said, looking sheepish, before cutting his eyes to Silas again, only to dip his head. "Guess I didn't exactly think that one through, huh?"

Jewel saw Silas take a deep, steadying breath. "How old are you again?"

"Fifteen."

Silas's gaze touched Jewel's before returning to her brother. "There's a futon in my family's shop, about a mile from here. You can crash there tonight. Go ahead and finish your meal, come get me in the living room when you're done, I'll drive you over."

After Silas left the room Aaron looked to her, his brows nearly meeting over his nose. "This isn't exactly working out the way I'd planned."

"Yeah, well, that's what happens when a person charges ahead with something when he's already been told *it won't work*. So you should consider yourself lucky to have someplace to sleep at all." Jewel stood to take his dish. "Silas was under no obligation to offer you even that much. You're none of his concern. That he did…" She walked over to the sink, realizing her hands were shaking. "Frankly," she said, turning, "I'd've put you on the first bus back to Denver."

"Really?" Aaron flashed her that wicked, dimpled smile that had instantly melted her heart when she'd first clapped eyes on the adorable two-year-old, and could still work its charm thirteen years later.

"No. *But*," she said when he laughed, "*only* because I don't have the money right now. This is serious, Aaron. And you sleeping on the futon in the Garretts' shop isn't even remotely close to a solution."

The kid's smile faded, even as his gaze swung to the leftover cake glittering like a trophy underneath the glass cover. Sighing, Jewel yanked a plate out of the cupboard and cut him a double slice.

"Thanks," he muttered, forking in a huge bite. Then he peered up at her from underneath his bangs. "You didn't finish your sentence."

"What sentence?"

"You said something about me being none of Silas's concern, then you said, 'That he did…'. That he did, what?"

"I can't remember," she lied, taking his already empty plate to cut him another slice, watching herself— once more—get sucked into something without her permission.

And she wasn't only talking about her brother.

Truth be told, Silas's first reaction when he'd seen Jewel pull the scrawny, sad sack kid into her arms was *Oh, hell no*. More responsibility, he did not need. But what was he gonna do? Toss the kid out on his butt?

Besides, once he got past the initial *Why me?*, Reaction Number Two clobbered him on the head, which was that if he wanted to go digging in Jewel's past, who better to hand him a map and shovel than her stepbrother?

Yeah. About that. In a week, tops, Jewel'd be out of his house, out of his life—except for the babysitting which was minimal contact—and all that stuff about it making him crazy unless he figured out what made her tick? It would fade. If he gave it half a chance. And/or told his brain to shut the hell up about it. Whatever was going on inside Jewel's head, it wasn't up to Silas to know, or fix, or make better.

Or her kid brother, sunk down with exhaustion in the seat next to him. Except Silas sensed Aaron was genuinely miserable, that he hadn't taken off on a lark, which naturally tugged at Silas's heart.

Even so, the boy shouldn't be rewarded for running away, nor did Jewel need that extra burden right now. Hence the futon offer. Not that sleeping in the office was like being consigned to hell: Silas, as well as all of his brothers, had all crashed on that futon at one time or another, for one reason or another, and lived to tell the tale. But the shop was what it was. And what it was, was several notches below a Motel 6.

"Your father even know where you are?" Silas said when they got inside and the kid dumped his backpack and bedroll onto the office's scuffed wood floor.

"Yeah, actually." He held up his phone. "GPS. Nice being tracked like some loser criminal, huh?"

"Considering what you did, not such a bad idea." The kid grimaced. "You need to at least tell him you're okay—"

"My father doesn't give a crap about me," the boy said quietly, plopping onto the edge of the futon and bouncing a little before popping back up to undo his sleeping bag, spread it out on the mattress. "And I'm not saying that because I'm some spoiled brat who's pissed because he didn't buy me the newest game system or something. He gives me everything I ask for. Except himself. It sucks, and I…" He swallowed. "I got tired of being last in line, okay?"

If the kid had snarled at him, or given him attitude, that would have been one thing. But he hadn't, which tamped down Silas's annoyance. He propped one hip on the desk, his hands linked on his lap.

"You pulled a fast one on your sister, though. That wasn't exactly cool."

"Yeah, I know." Aaron shoved his long fingers, the nails chewed to the quick, through his stringy hair. "But I didn't know what else to do."

"What about your mother?"

"She died when I was little. I never even knew her." The sleeping bag arranged to his satisfaction, he flopped on it, his skate shoes thudding to the floor when he toed them off. He leaned over to drag another hoodie out of his backpack, wadding it up and stuffing it behind his head. "Jewel was the closest I ever got to somebody acting like my mom. When her mom and my dad split, I felt like somebody'd punched me in the gut."

Ah, hell. It was everything Silas could do not to yank the kid into his arms himself. "But she's only, what? Nine, ten years older than you?"

Aaron wriggled around to prop his head in his hand. "Yeah. I know. But it was her who cooked and cleaned and stuff, who came into my room at night when I got scared. Who took me to school and helped me with my homework. Dude—she took care of me. She cared about me. Nobody else did. Ever. So now…"

His Adam's apple working, he shook his head. "I didn't know where else to go. I know we're not related by blood or anything, but she's, like all I've got. Hey—" Spotting the computer, he bounced upright again. "You got wireless? 'Cause I could totally gank your signal for my laptop."

Silas pushed himself away from the desk. "Knock yourself out. On one condition."

"What's that?"

"Call your father. Maybe it doesn't matter to him," he said when the boy opened his mouth, "but it matters to Jewel. And me."

"Okay, fine. Whatever. But it won't make any difference."

Thinking, *And this is what I have to look forward to,* Silas walked to the door. "It shouldn't get too cold in here, but there's a space heater if it does. Just turn it off when you go to sleep. Somebody'll come get you for breakfast around seven-thirty. And..."

And, what? This wasn't his problem to solve.

Yeah. Say it another hundred times or so, and maybe you'll actually believe it.

"And we'll figure out what comes next," he said. "'Night."

"'Night. Silas?"

He twisted back. "Yeah?"

His laptop already open, the kid looked up, his face silver in the glow from the computer screen. "I know this has nothing to do with you. So I really, really appreciate you not kicking me to the curb or anything. Seriously, thanks. And if there's anything I can do to, like, return the favor? I'm totally cool with that."

"You're welcome," Silas said after a moment. "Although you might want to wait to see what we decide before you thank me. See you in the morning."

When he got back, Jewel was still at the kitchen table, her head in her hands. He thought at first she'd been crying, but when she lifted her head she was dry-eyed, her brows drawn behind her glasses. Obviously miffed, but not a basket case. Then Silas thought about what Aaron had said, about her being the only mother figure he'd ever had, and he thought, *Gotcha*.

Except, somehow, it felt a helluva lot more like he was the one who'd been caught.

Chapter Eight

"I'm so, so sorry about this," Jewel said before Silas could open his mouth.

Silas looked at her for a long moment, then moseyed over to the cake platter, cutting himself another piece and plunking it on a napkin. "I'm a lot more sorry about *this*," he muttered around a bite, dripping crumbs all over his shirt. "Triple Temptation, you should call it."

Jewel smiled, but it wasn't her normal puppies and rainbows smile. And it faded fast. "Oh, Lord, Silas…first my mother, then Aaron, both in the same day…so not fair."

"To which one of us?"

She burbled out a laugh. "Both." Then she sighed. "I called Aaron's dad while you were gone."

"Oh? And?"

"Went straight to voice mail. I mean, if it was your kid, wouldn't you be jumping on the phone the minute it rang?

Or calling *his* cell? Geezy Pete—what is *wrong* with that man?"

Her obvious worry about someone she hadn't seen since she was sixteen, who wasn't even a blood relative, cut Silas to the quick. Then it struck him, especially when he considered her extremely charitable attitude toward her mother, that there wasn't a soul on earth more loyal than Jewel Jasper. That when she loved, she loved like a child—deep and forever and unconditionally.

Not helping, he thought, the bite of cake clogging his throat. He grabbed some child's leftover milk from dinner and gulped it down.

"You really care about the kid, don't you?"

A small, heartbreaking smile touched her mouth, and he wanted to hold her so badly it made him dizzy. "Probably way more than I should."

"No such thing. Sounds like he's damn lucky to have you in his life."

She blushed. "You're sweet to say so, but what good am I to him right now? Especially if I have to send him back…" Cradling her head in her hands, she muttered, "I have no earthly idea how to fix this."

"And maybe you should go on to bed and we'll talk about it in the morning—"

"This isn't your problem, Silas!" Straightening her glasses, she blew her nose into a napkin. "Oh, Lord, if I'd had any idea…" Her mouth flat, she met his gaze, her own an odd combination of confusion, vexation and determination. "The last thing I wanted, or expected, when I accepted either of your offers was for you to get sucked into my family dramas. I keep thinking you must be having some serious regrets, right about now. You want me to make other arrangements, I'd completely understand—"

Without thinking, Silas reached across the table and

grabbed her hand. Not the smartest move he could've made, considering the *zzzzt* that practically made him lurch, both at her touch and the way her eyes latched on to his in response, but too late now.

"And you can stop that train of thought right now. You're not going anywhere. Unless you want to." After a moment, she slowly shook her head and Silas released her hand. "Besides, you got a hefty dose of my parents tonight, too. I think we can call it even."

Tucking her hands into her crossed arms, she smiled. "You may have a point. Although there's a big difference between cooking a little dinner and suddenly having a runaway on your hands. And I repeat—this is my problem. Not yours."

Silas settled back in his chair, considering how much he should say. Finally he settled on, "When's the last time you had anybody there for *you?*"

Her gaze instantly sharpened. "What do you mean?"

"Aaron told me you as good as raised him when you were kids. That for all intents and purposes you were his mom."

Jewel flushed, then gave a nervous laugh. "He was exaggerating, he was far too little to remember…"

"Then you didn't do all the cooking and laundry? You weren't the one who comforted him when he had a bad dream?"

Her cheeks got so bright he half expected them to combust. "I was only doing what needed to be done. And it wasn't like I minded. Keeping everything in order, being who Aaron came to when he was scared or sad…it made me feel good. Like…"

"Like you mattered?"

"No! Okay—" she toyed with one of her earrings "—maybe deep down that was partly true, although I don't

remember thinking about myself at the time. All I wanted
was to see him happy. And you know as well as I do there's
no better feeling on earth than when a little kid trusts you.
So…maybe it did make me feel like I mattered. Mattered
to *him*."

"And he wasn't the only one you took care of, was
he?"

When her eyes lowered, Silas reached for her hand again.
"I knew there was something screwy about what you said
earlier, when you gave me that song and dance about how
you had never really grown up because your mother hadn't.
In fact, the opposite was true, wasn't it? Not the part about
your mother's immaturity—I've met the woman, there's no
denying that—but it wasn't that you never had a chance to
grow up. It was that you grew up too soon."

Her eyes glanced off his before she got up to cover the
cake again. Oddly encouraged by her silence—at least she
wasn't denying it—Silas pushed further. "What I'm not
understanding, is why the act?"

Her gaze jerked to his. "Act?"

"Yeah. No damn way are you a space cadet. But something tells me you want people to think you are. I don't get
it."

Jewel scraped the frosting off the knife blade with her
index finger, sticking the goo in her mouth before dropping
the knife into the dishwasher. "Liking to have fun doesn't
make me a space cadet," she said softly.

"The Beanie Babies?"

She almost smiled, only to slide to the floor to hug the
dog, not even trying to dodge The Tongue. "You know,
sometimes I think the world would be a much better place if
more people let themselves act like kids from time to time. I
don't mean shirking their responsibilities, or not being able

to function on their own. But being able to simply *enjoy* life without analyzing everything to death."

"Believe it or not, I agree," Silas said quietly, hurting for her, for what had been so rudely taken from her. "The world does need more of that. But that's not what I'm talking about. Which you know."

She glanced up. "It's just easier that way."

"What's easier?"

"Life. My life, anyway."

"Still not getting it, honey."

After a long, considering look, she got up and shuffled back to the table to drop into the chair again. "Okay, you're right, I was the caretaker in my family from the time I was old enough to run the washer and reach the stove. I honestly don't know if I picked up the slack because I wanted Mama to notice me, I was genuinely afraid I'd starve to death or because I'm a nurturer. All three, I suppose. However…"

She took a deep breath. "I love my mother, Silas. And I know she loves me. But somewhere along the way it hit me I'd become a doormat. That I was enabling Mama—not that I knew the term at the time, but that was the truth of it—by doing everything for her so she wouldn't have to. Even after I'd had my little revelation, though, it was simply easier to stick with the status-quo than to try to change things. Change her. Finally it occurred to me that was never going to happen—for either of us—unless I left."

And he could see it in her eyes, that the decision had nearly killed her. "When was this?" he asked gently.

"The epiphany? When I was still in high school. Couldn't get away, though, until college. We were living in Las Cruces then. I think—we lived so many places it's hard to remember—but I 'escaped' to Albuquerque when I got a scholarship to UNM nursing school."

"And your mother?"

"Moved to Albuquerque to be closer to me."

"Damn."

She smirked. "Yeah. And sure enough, every time I'd try to assert myself, tell her I had plans, she'd always get to me, and I'd feel bad for her and drop whatever I was doing to go help her, or hang out with her…and we'd be right back at square one. So after I graduated I moved up to Billings to work in a hospital there."

"And she didn't follow you?"

"Amazingly enough, no. She'd started coaching baby skaters by then, had a good thing going in Albuquerque, so she stayed put."

"So when did Justin happen?"

She almost smiled. "Caught that, didja? My senior year of college. I'll admit I was temporarily blinded by the *idea* of being married, and Justin's a nice enough guy, but…" She shrugged. "I wasn't ready. Fortunately I realized that before I made a huge mistake. I think Mama took it worse than Justin."

"So I gathered."

"Anyway, while I was in Billings I shared a house with a midwife who did home births and who'd apprenticed with Patrice several years ago—which is how I ended up back here—as well as with a recently divorced family therapist who was only too happy to let me babble to her in exchange for a decent meal."

She tugged the ponytail holder out of her hair, massaging her scalp where it had been. "I already knew how lopsided I'd let my life get, but she helped me see that it's one thing to be giving, another thing entirely to give until the well runs dry without clue one how to fill it up again. Not to mention that because I've never actually been part of a balanced relationship? I have no idea how one goes about that.

"So the consensus was I needed to do two things. One, continue to stay out of my mother's way as much as possible, even if kills me, until she either learns to stand on her own two feet, which I'm not holding my breath about, or until I can be her daughter without being her lackey."

She held his gaze until Silas felt the weight of whatever she was about to say somehow shift to him.

"And the other?"

"Avoid romantic entanglements until I find that balance. Until I figure out how to make *Jewel* happy before I lose myself again by trying so hard to make somebody else happy. Only thing is, it's been three years, and I don't feel any closer to understanding what the heck any of that means than I did then." She paused, then said softly, "*Now* do you get it?"

Yeah. Right between the eyes. Not that her words surprised him. His reaction, though, threw him for a major loop. "That still doesn't explain the act, though."

"Sure it does. Because I did learn *something* from observing my mother—that while some men find the giggly, helpless routine amusing, most don't. And even those who do get tired of it pretty quickly." Her shoulders hitched. "It's a useful…tool."

"You act goofy on purpose to keep men at bay?"

"The serious ones, anyway."

"Meaning guys who are serious in general, or ones who might be serious about you?"

Another small shrug preceded, "Either. Both."

Silence thrummed between them.

"And…which one was I?"

She smiled. Sort of. "Oh, come on, Silas—it's like using a seat belt—doesn't mean you're gonna get in an accident, just something you do automatically. In case."

He could have left it there, strangled in its seat belt

metaphor. But he didn't. Oh, no, just had to poke at it by saying, "Except now I know. That you're pretending."

"Ah, but you also know why I was. So nothing's changed, right? Come on, the last thing *you* need in your life is some chick with more issues than *TIME Magazine*. Far as I can tell, I'm as safe with you as I'd be with Santa Claus."

Depends on who's wearing the Santa suit. "Can't argue with that logic," Silas said, feeling unaccountably grumpy. "However, there is one tiny glitch in your logic you may have overlooked."

"And what's that?"

"Actually, two things. One, that being a giver isn't a liability. Or a character flaw. Not as long as you give because you want to, and not because you're trying to get something in return. And two," he added before she could wedge in an objection, "I'm no more capable of looking the other way, of not lending a hand when it's needed, than you are. For good or bad, it's who I am. What I do. Which means if you think you have to handle this situation with Aaron all by yourself, you're dead wrong."

"I see," she said. Silas couldn't tell if she was amused or pissed. Probably both. "And what if I don't want your help?"

"You're outta luck. You want to find balance? First step is to let somebody else share the load. And if you don't," he said, standing, "you'll have to answer to my mother. And I don't think either one of us want *that*."

After another long moment Jewel cracked up laughing. Then—get this—she got up and wrapped her arms around his waist to give him a hug, before heading back to her room.

Leaving Silas standing there, wondering what the hell had just happened.

And worse, what the hell came next.

* * *

Jewel had barely walked into the kitchen the next morning when a knock at the back door scared the bejeebers out of her. God knew she was already jittery as all get-out on account of getting maybe a total of three hours sleep the night before, thanks to both her idiot brother and the even bigger idiot whose houseguest she was.

Pressing her pounding heart back into place, she shoved aside the flimsy window curtain to see Aaron doing a rapid, stiff-handed wave, his grin all but hidden by the breath cloud masking his face.

"Thanks for shaving five years off my life," she said, barely getting out of his way as he shoved his way inside to dump his gear on the floor beside Doughboy's water dish. "How on earth did you get here? One of us would've picked you up later."

Even though he was shivering like mad, Aaron went straight to the fridge and grabbed a carton of orange juice. "I'm about to starve. Besides, it was fricking freezing in that shop and the heater didn't work. So I walked over here. What's for breakfast?"

"I'll let you know once I've woken up. And for pity's sake!" Jewel swiped the carton from him a split-second before the open spout reached his mouth. "That's disgusting! Here." She plunked a glass in front of him and poured juice into it. "Welcome to civilization—"

"Aaron?" Silas said, shrugging into an old leather jacket as he came into the kitchen. "Did Jewel go get you…? Oh." His gaze scraped her jammies and ratty robe. Her uncombed hair. Yeah, she was ready for her photo shoot, all righty. One side of his mouth tilted up and her stomach went flippity flop. "I'm guessing not."

How was it, she wondered, that two people could have a lengthy conversation about why nothing was going to happen between them—whether those actual words were used or not—only to have said conversation somehow turn and bite them both in the butt? At least, hers certainly had chomp marks on it. Whether Silas's did or not, she couldn't say. For sure.

Then he did the gaze-scraping thing again, and she thought, *Oh, for heaven's sake—I look like hell on a bad day! Get over it!* and as if he could read her mind his grin stretched a little farther, and she knew her sleepless night had not been without cause.

What on *earth* had possessed her to admit she'd been playing the airhead on purpose to throw Silas off the scent? All that folderol about seat belts notwithstanding.

"Pancakes okay with everybody?" she said, slamming the griddle onto the burner, making all parties present flinch, including the dog, which only seemed fair considering the state they'd put her in. Except for the dog.

"Yeah, sure—"

"Cool."

Because for *hours* she'd lain awake with one word scrolling across her brain like those dumb CNN headlines at the bottom of the TV screen: Why…why….why…?

Why had she blabbed like that? And why to Silas? And why, why did Silas care? And why did she care, whether Silas cared or not?

One seriously messed up chick to go, please.

Deciding she'd clobber with the griddle the next person dumb enough to initiate early-morning banter, she got out pancake ingredients, made batter, slapped syrup and plates and flatware on the table, made pancakes, served pancakes, and drank copious amounts of coffee whilst glaring at the two males at the kitchen table. Who, it pained her to note, seemed either unaware of her grumpiness or were taking great pains to ignore it.

Nothing worse than an unappreciated snit.

Then, noticing the time, she went in to rouse Ollie. Not because she had to, but because small, sweet, sleepy boys—even groggy, grouchy ones—were far preferable to the big, heartbreaking, wide-awake ones currently yukking it up over her pancakes.

Okay, they weren't exactly yukking it up. In fact, the conversation sounded pretty darned serious. A conversation *she* should be having with her brother, not Silas. And would, as soon as she had a chance. And yet...

"Go 'way," Ollie now mumbled, burrowing farther underneath his covers. "I'm sleepy."

Sitting on the edge of his bed, Jewel curled herself around the little boy, gently tickling him through two inches of polyester fiber filling. "I know, sugar, but you have to get ready for school."

"Don'wannagotoschool."

"There's pancakes."

One eye peeked over the comforter edge, underneath a fan of electrified blond hair. "With choc'late chips? And whipped cream?"

"Only if you get to the table by the time..." She tapped her finger on the face of the digital clock by his bed. "The number on this side of the dots turns to ten."

"Pancakes?" Tad bellowed from across the room, his covers flying as he scrambled out of bed and charged across the hall to the bathroom.

"Hey! Me, first!" Ollie said, stomping after him, where the boys held a brief battle for first toilet rights—Jewel did not want to know—before they torpedoed back to their respective dressers for clean clothes. Or, in Ollie's case, the jumble of jeans, hoodies and T-shirts beside his bed—Silas's single concession to messy, apparently. A second later Tad appeared in front of her, apparently no match for the buttons on his western-style shirt.

She drew him closer, her heart squeezing at his puckered frown, then his sweet, baby-toothed smile as she showed him how to guide the slippery buttons through the holes. "Did it, yay!" he shouted, pumping his fist, then taking a swing at his brother, just because he could. A swing that was reciprocated, naturally, and then they were wrassling in the pile of clothes, the dog barking and trying to get in on the act, honestly, until Jewel waded into the fracas to redirect their energy into pulling their beds together and getting their shoes on.

And she thought about how patient Silas was with these two fireballs, what a good father he was—what a good man, period—and that *if* she'd been in the market for a husband and potential father of her own hypothetical children, if *he'd* been in the market for a potential stepmom for the ones he already had, he'd definitely be in the running.

Even so, as she broke up yet another tussle—seriously considering rubbing them down with dryer sheets to keep them from clinging to each other—she thought about what Silas had said about her needing to learn how to let somebody else take care of her. But the thing was, what he didn't understand—what nobody did—was that it wasn't that she didn't know *how* to let somebody else take care of her.

It was how much it hurt when they stopped.

Silas watched the teen inhale his pancakes as if buzzards were circling overhead, waiting to swoop. His plate clean, he cast a longing glance at the stove. "Is there more?"

"There's batter and a griddle. Have at it."

His gaze swung to Silas's. "Uh…cooking's not exactly my thing? Ramen and pop-tarts is pretty much my limit."

"Then this is your lucky day."

"Why can't I wait for Jewel? Be…cause," he said at Silas's you-get-one-guess look, "she's in a really bad mood?"

"That would be it. Go on, I'll talk you through it. You call your Dad?" Silas asked as, with a huge *why-me?* breath, Aaron dragged himself over to the stove.

"Yeah. His cell and the landline, got voice mail both times. What's first?"

"Give the griddle a squirt of the cooking spray, put the flame on medium high, wait until the griddle begins to smoke. Did you try each phone more than once?"

Shaggy hair bounced when he nodded. "I told you he doesn't care…okay, it's smoking. Next?"

"Pour the batter onto the griddle?"

"Oh. Yeah." The griddle sizzled. "How do I know when to flip 'em?"

"When the bubbles have all popped and the pancakes look dry around the edges."

Eyes glued to the pancakes, Aaron slouched in front of the stove, one hand stuffed in the pocket of his droopy cargo pants, the other tapping the spatula against the edge of the counter. "Jewel's mad because of me, huh?"

Among other things, Silas imagined. Like, for instance, that hormone-riddled do-si-do at the end of their little talk last night. Then to give her that once-over a few minutes ago…

Dumb.

"You showing up like this isn't exactly making her life easier, no," Silas said, and the boy banged the spatula harder.

"She's…different than I expected. In some ways, any-way."

"Last time you saw her," Silas pointed out, "she was

barely older than you are now. Big difference between sixteen and twenty-five."

"Yeah, I know. In my head, anyway. But I thought…I dunno. I guess I figured she could still make things better somehow. Like she always used to. Stupid, huh?"

"And trust me, if she could, she would. Even so…" Silas picked up the gaming magazine the boy had been leafing through as he ate, only to put it back down when he realized it may as well have been written in Sanskrit. "It sounds like she's been taking care of other people her whole life. Don't you think it's time she took care of herself?"

More banging. Then: "Yeah, maybe you're right. Doesn't solve my problem, though."

"True. But that doesn't mean we can't."

That got a funny look. "We?"

"You're in my house, eating my pancakes." Silas shrugged. "So, yeah. *We*."

Aaron grinned, then turned back to the griddle. A few seconds later, Silas heard the scrape of spatula against Teflon, followed by, "Dude! Looks like a real pancake and everything! And…whoo-hoo! Did it again. Hey—you think it'd be okay if I make some for the kids since I'm on a roll, here?"

"Go for it."

Soon after, said kids vroomed into the kitchen, spilling half their already-poured juice as they chugged it down. "Jewel said there's pancakes?" Tad asked around Silas's taking a napkin to the child's mouth and chin.

"Yeah," she said as she reappeared, still a mess. Still cute. Still, he was guessing, grouchy. "Just give me a minute—"

"Already done," Aaron said, plunking piled plates in front of each child. Of course, then the boys scrapped over who got the syrup and whipped cream first, until Jewel grabbed both out of their hands with an amazingly strong *"Hey!"* for such a wee thing, giving them the same look he'd seen a million times on his mother's face, after which they planted their bottoms back on their chairs.

"Dudes," Aaron said, shaking his head as he forked in another bite. "Trust me, that's a 'pull that again and you won't see pancakes again until you're eighty' look."

Coughing to cover his laugh, Silas pushed away from the table and carried his plate to the sink. "Impressive," he whispered to Jewel, standing two feet away as she refilled her coffee cup.

"Kids need limits," she said quietly, not looking at him, both hands clamped around her mug as she sipped. "Chaos sucks."

"Or rules, depending on your point of view."

Blowing a short laugh through her nose, she almost smiled. But he could tell she was an inch away from buckling underneath this new pressure. He also knew she'd cut off a limb before admitting it.

"C'n we have more whipped cream, Jewel?" Ollie asked, twisted around in his chair and peeking through the rungs like a caged monkey. "We'll be good, promise."

"Yeah. Promise," Tad added, nodding like a bobble-head.

Jewel cast Silas a bemused glance, then turned, clearly as much of a softie as Silas. "Okay…but only a little. No, let Aaron do it," she said, adding more milk to the batter to stretch it for her own breakfast.

"You do realize," Silas said as whoops of approval masked the sound of Aaron's smothering the pancakes with whipped cream, "your brother's take on 'a little' probably doesn't match yours?"

"Don't be so sure about that," she said, only her joke fell flatter than the puny pancakes on the griddle.

"Jewel—?"

"What am I gonna do with him?" she said softly, achingly, flooding her pancakes with syrup. Then she turned, leaning against the counter to eat them, watching Aaron goof around with Silas's two like they'd all known each other forever. "If Keith really is as uncaring as Aaron says…" She shook her head, her eyes lowered, before lifting them again to Silas. "He's my heart, Silas. Has been from the first moment I laid eyes on him. And I look at him now," she said, returning her gaze to the giggling boys, "and I think…that's what he should have had all along. Or something close to it, at least. A *real* family. Not a succession of so-called parents who dragged their kids behind them like…"

She didn't, or couldn't, finish her sentence. Not that she had to.

"He's a good kid," she said after a moment. "He deserves better. And it *kills* me that I can't give that to him."

Ah, hell. At that moment, the only thing keeping Silas from taking her into his arms was their audience. But when she set her empty plate on the counter, he did reach for her hand, earning him a very startled glance that dovetailed nicely with his own reaction—that her openness, her honesty, her uncompromising integrity were breaching defenses he'd assumed were virtually impenetrable even a few weeks before. That her being here felt so good, so *right,* as though…

"You have one of the biggest hearts of anyone I've ever met," he said, holding her gaze captive in his. Then he let go. You know, before the moment turned awkward. Before he said something really stupid, like about how she deserved better, too. About how, maybe, he could do something about that, if she let him.

Because it hadn't taken but a second for surprise to turn

to wariness to turn to something close to terror in her eyes, that his simple gesture of concern and support might mean something…more. Something she couldn't possibly deal with right now. Maybe not ever.

Oh, yeah, he understood that look, all right. All too well. Since not that long ago he'd been right there with her in No Damn Way Land. But how could he watch her with his kids, with her brother—heck, with anyone she came in contact with—and not think it might be nice to have her compassion and grace and courage and, yes, craziness in his life, in his kids' lives, on a regular basis?

"Thank you," she said with one of those tiny smiles, then looked away, once more cradling her coffee mug in her hands. "Except that big heart is exactly what keeps getting me in trouble."

Silas stared at her profile for a long moment, knowing he should respond but having no earthly idea what to say that wouldn't sound trite. Or like he was brushing off her fears as silly. So instead he called Ollie to get his jacket and go out to the car.

"I'll check in at lunch," he said, digging his keys out of his pocket, "but you need anything before then? You call me. Promise?"

"You bet," she said.

But without anything even remotely resembling eye contact.

Chapter Nine

"Hey," Aaron said an hour later as they traipsed through the woods, Tad bopping along well ahead of them while Doughboy lumbered along beside, periodically giving Jewel sad sack *Can we stop now? Now? How about now?* looks. "Does Silas, like, have a thing for you?"

And, yep, that would be her heart trying to escape her chest. "No! What makes you think that?"

"Uh, the way he looks at you?"

Despite her sour mood, Jewel barked out a laugh. "You mean, the 'What planet are you from?' look?"

"No, the 'I really like this chick but have no clue how to tell her' look."

"You're fifteen, what do you know?"

Now Aaron laughed, his deep voice all squeaky-new. "Yeah. Fifteen. Not *five*. Trust me, I know that look."

"And I'm so not having this conversation with you," Jewel said, linking her hands around his elbow, willing herself to believe that concentrating on the crisp, woodsmoke scented air, the serene blue sky and glittering sunlight playing peek-a-boo with the yellowing live oaks and aspens would wipe that…that…okay, that *look* in Silas's eyes out of her head.

Because that look could get her into one big, steaming heap o' trouble, if she let it.

He thought *she* had a big heart? Ohmigosh—if she lived to be a hundred she'd never live down how badly she'd misjudged him at first. The difference was, he was smart enough to hang on to his. She wasn't. Or at least it was a lot harder for her, given her history and nature and all…her firm resolve notwithstanding. So for sure she was counting on Silas to be the good guy and keep a lid on his self control, because too many more of those smoldering looks, those not-so-random acts of kindness, and there was no telling what she might do—

And, hello? She was supposed to be focusing on solving her brother's dilemma, not mooning over a hot, sweet geek whose touch that morning had sent her core temperature soaring farther and faster than—

Stop that!

A contented sigh floated over her head. "This place is awesome. Where's the high school?"

"You've been here like five minutes, you'd be bored out of your skull in five more, and you can't stay. Your father—"

"Still not picking up."

Jewel's pocket suddenly R2-D2'd at her. She dug out her phone, surprised to see Gene Garrett's name on the display.

"Silas gave me your cell number," Donna said. "I hope you don't mind—"

"No, of course not—"

"—but I cannot fit one more casserole in my freezer. I love my church sisters to death, I really do, but they simply do not know when to quit with the food! So I asked Silas if y'all might like to take some of this stuff off my hands, and he said you could pop on over sometime and get it?"

"Um, sure. I'll be there in a bit."

"What was that all about?" Aaron asked when she slipped her phone back into her pocket and called Tad to come back.

"Silas's mom and overzealous church ladies," Jewel said, adding, when Aaron frowned at her, "all will be made clear in a few minutes."

"See?" Donna said, opening both her refrigerator and freezer doors, revealing Tupperware and covered foil pans as far as the eye could see. "I wasn't kidding. And that's not counting what I've got stashed in the big freezer out in the garage."

"Holy...cow."

"Not exactly what I said, but close. Honestly, you'd think I'd *died.*"

Jewel sputtered a laugh, as, behind them at the kitchen table, Aaron and Tad chowed down big slabs of somebody's homemade coffee cake, shoved in front of them the minute they set foot in the door. More agile now that she was used to the walking boot, Donna began unloading the fridge, setting tray after tray on the other end of the table with appropriate commentary for each one.

"Okay, you probably don't want Mildred's macaroni and cheese—I don't know what she does to it, it's like eating solid lard, but I simply don't have the heart to toss it. Yet. Oh...this one's not bad, it's something Sally Perkins calls Greek Chicken, it's got that feta cheese on it. Which I like but Gene wouldn't eat if it was the only thing in the house.

And this one's…oh, yes—Emma Manning's green chili stew—"

"Oh! I've had that, when Patrice and I went up there before she had her baby? It's really good."

"Then you take it, green chili and Gene don't see eye-to-eye anymore…."

After another ten minutes or so spent divvying the largesse between them—and after the boys finished their snack and Tad took Aaron off to show him Gene's two-thousand-and-counting Hot Wheels collection—Donna lowered her ample form into one of the chairs and cut Jewel a big old slab of coffee cake, the cream cheese icing gleaming in the morning sun slanting across the table. No sooner had she slid it in front of Jewel, though, than she glanced over her shoulder to make sure the boys were still out of ear-shot and whispered, "Silas told me about your stepbrother's surprise appearance. Land, boys will get the craziest ideas in their heads, won't they? You want coffee with that?"

"Please. And yes, they do. This went above and beyond, though."

"Honey," Donna said as she poured coffee into two mugs, "if I had a nickel for every lamebrained thing my guys did growing up, I'd be wealthier than Bill Gates. Half-and-half okay?" When Jewel nodded, she set the carton on the table, along with the sugar bowl, then lowered herself again into the chair, stirring two spoonfuls of sugar into her own coffee. "Have you decided what to do?"

"Working on it," Jewel said, even though the answer was a flat-out "no." Her throat closed, refusing admission to the cake. On a soft, commiserating moan, Donna reached over to curl her fingers around Jewel's.

"I'm sure there's a solution," she said, giving Jewel's

hand a firm squeeze before releasing it. "There always is, if you get quiet long enough to listen for the answer."

Why couldn't you have been my mother? Jewel thought, which she realized was both pointless and mean, provoking a spurt of guilt that further obstructed the coffee cake's journey.

"Yes, ma'am. I'm trying to do that, but…" The mug shook slightly when she lifted it to her lips.

Donna reached inside her sweater pocket for a folded tissue. "Go ahead, it's clean, I only put it there this morning." Nodding, Jewel blew her nose, wiped her eyes under her glasses, then took off the glasses to clean the smudges. Silas's mother smiled. "Nobody ever said trusting was easy."

Then she inclined her head toward the laughter coming down the hall. "God knows there were times our boys nearly sent us over the edge, but I find myself missing that period of our lives more often than not. Teenage boys are a hoot and a half." Her eyes swung back to Jewel's. "And Aaron seems like a good boy."

"Except for the running away thing, you mean?" Jewel said with a smile as, determined, she renewed her assault on the hapless pastry. "Yeah. I couldn't love him more if we were blood relations."

"I can see that." Sympathetic eyes met hers. "But right now you no more need a teenager to look after than I need a dozen more casseroles."

Despite the still threatening tears, Jewel laughed, the laughter dwindling to nothing when Donna added, "And you do not need to feel guilty about that. Love him or not, taking on a responsibility that's not yours is only asking for trouble."

Donna's insight was making Jewel even wobblier, which would never do. "Oh, I absolutely agree. Besides, Aaron belongs with his daddy. And I'm sure this is nothing more than a big misunderstanding. Keith's...okay."

And wasn't that a rousing endorsement of the man? True, her memories of those years maybe weren't as sharp as they should be, but she was pretty sure she'd recall if there'd been problems. Aside from those between Keith and Mama, that is. Those, she'd remember to her dying day. "Not that Keith was around all that much. He traveled a lot for his job, installing computer systems for big companies. I think."

"Good money in that line of work, I hear."

"I suppose, I wouldn't really know." Frowning, Jewel lightly tapped her fork on the rim of her plate. "I gather Aaron's spent a lot of time with housekeepers and such. Which makes it even more important he be with his dad as much as possible while he's still in school, right? But why hasn't Keith returned any of our messages? I can't imagine he's not worried sick about Aaron. It simply doesn't add up—"

At Donna's quick head shake, Jewel clamped shut her mouth. A second later the boys trooped back into the kitchen, Aaron declaring Gene's miniature car collection totally awesome. Then, noticing Donna's struggle to fit whatever she was keeping back into the fridge, he immediately jumped in to help, earning him one of Donna's super-duper hugs.

And the kid ate it up, which only further mangled Jewel's heart.

So it really wasn't a surprise that, on the way back to the house, a weirdly silent Aaron sank down in the front seat, his head propped against the car window.

"Whatcha thinking?" Jewel asked.

He rustled in his seat, then scrubbed his palm over his knee. "Is Silas's dad as cool as his mom?"

Jewel smiled. "Depends on your definition of that, I

suppose, but yeah. I like Gene a lot. Although after rais-ing Silas and his brothers? Nothing gets past either one of 'em… Aaron?" He'd twisted around in his seat, muttering a bad word under his breath. "Is the sheriff tailing me or something?"

"Not the sheriff," he said, jerking back around and slid-ing down in his seat. When he finally looked over at her, he'd gone practically the same color as his gray hoodie. "My dad."

The silence—relative silence, anyway—when Silas re-turned to the house around four immediately tipped him off that something was very, very wrong. Over a jolt of ap-prehension, he walked into the living room, where he found an oddly subdued Jewel curled up on the sofa, watching the boys vroom-vroom their Tonka fleet on the floor in front of her.

"Hey," he said softly, which brought her face up to his, even as Tad jumped up to launch himself at Silas's thighs.

"Aaron's daddy came and took him away!" he said, and Silas's eyes shot back to Jewel's.

"You're kidding?"

Shaking her head, she unfolded herself to lower her feet to the floor, her fingers gripping the edge of the sofa as she gave him a tight, gonna-keep-it-together-if-it-kills-me smile. "Keith showed up right before lunch. They left al-most immediately."

And if that wasn't an extremely abridged version of events, he didn't know what was. Especially when Tad chirped, "There was a lot of yelling, too! His daddy called Aaron a—"

"Tadpole!" Jewel said, her face red as a radish, at which point Silas—who was jumping to conclusions about Aaron's father faster than a grasshopper ahead of a wildfire—dragged out his phone and asked Mrs. Maple if she wouldn't mind a couple little visitors for a few minutes.

When he returned from hauling his scowling, protesting sons to the neighbor's, Jewel was still perched where he'd left her, only now her arms were folded tightly across her middle as she stared blankly across the room. "Just when I think things can't get worse," she whispered, not looking at Silas, "they do."

"Unfortunately, a feeling I know all too well," he said gently. "What happened?"

"It was horrible," she said in a tiny voice. "K-Keith pulled up behind us and jumped out of his car, practically dragging Aaron out of mine and lighting into him right there in the driveway. It all happened so fast, I barely had a chance to get Tad inside. And even after I did, Keith was so loud I could hear him through the windows calling his own son an idiot, saying he'd be s-sorry he'd ever pulled a stunt like this…."

On a sob, she buried her face in her hands, and Silas was across the room in three strides to pull her into his arms, covering her fisted hands on his chest with one of his own. "Then Aaron stormed inside to get his stuff…. and ohmigod, the look he gave me, Silas! And I couldn't do a blessed thing to h-help him!"

For a moment Silas shut his eyes, riding out the breath-stealing sense of déjà-vu.

"Why didn't you call me?"

"I never had a chance. And for Tad's sake I didn't want to make an even b-bigger deal out of it than it was."

His youngest son had told him, on the way to Mrs. Maple's, how Jewel had taken care of them "like everything was okay," after Aaron had gone. That she'd made lunch and played with him, helped him practice his letters and numbers, even taken him and Ollie out for a short bike ride when Ollie got home from school. Meaning, for four *hours* she'd pretended things were perfectly normal when she was obviously a wreck inside.

In contrast, Amy had called him in hysterics over every minor crisis. And how often had Ollie met him at the door with "Mommy cried because the baby got powder all over us," or "Mommy got mad because I tried to get some milk and spilled it all over"? The list of Things That Set Mommy Off was seemingly endless.

This gal, though, was clearly built of sterner stuff. No wussy little bunny rabbit here, boy, Silas thought with a small smile, then planted a brief kiss on her head without any thought at all. Jewel stiffened, then bounced up from the couch and hotfooted it to the kitchen.

"Lord, I must look a sight," she said, ripping a paper towel off the roller by the sink and dampening it under a stream of water before removing her glasses to press the wet wad to each eye in turn.

"You look fine," Silas said, getting to his feet and crossing to the breakfast bar, suddenly realizing how huge her eyes were without her glasses. How she averted those eyes, like there was something more. Something she wasn't telling him. Sliding onto a stool, Silas folded his hands in front of him. "Now tell me the parts you left out."

She lowered the paper towel, gawking. "What makes you think there's more?"

"Call it a hunch, okay?" he said, figuring a little irritation in his voice might get the point across, that he cared.

And no, he had no idea where, if anywhere, he was going with that. The future would take care of itself, as the future had been doing forever. But right now the only thing that mattered was that Jewel Jasper knew he gave a damn about her.

That *somebody* did.

"But Mrs. M—"

"Is fine. The boys are fine. You're not. So you may as well start talking because I'm not going anywhere."

Her heart knocking against her ribs, Jewel did the rabbit-in-the-hunter's-sights thing with Silas, having no earthly idea what the heck had just happened.

Until she came to her senses and realized, *Oh, right—that would be pity, got it,* except then Silas's eyes went all squinchy and suspicious behind his glasses as if he was reading her mind and didn't like what he saw, so she amended *pity* to *compassion,* which was only a higher-falutin way of saying *feeling sorry for.*

Which obviously accounted for all that huggy stuff on his sofa.

Not to mention the kiss on her head.

Then she did a whole-body shiver which served to shake loose any inclination to read anything else into the hugs and the kiss, as Silas said, "So how did Keith find Aaron, anyway?"

Deep breath time. Letting him think she was slightly spacey was one thing, coming across as a complete wimp something else entirely.

"Apparently through that GPS thing on Aaron's phone. So he really had known where he was all the time." Spying the still-cooling chocolate chip cookies she and the boys had baked earlier, she grabbed a spatula, slid a half dozen onto a plate and set it in front of Silas before taking one herself. "He said he'd half thought of 'letting the boy rot'—his words—then changed his mind. What makes me sick, though, is that he obviously hadn't come because he was worried about Aaron, he was just mad. Mad that Aaron had pulled one over on him, mad that *he'd* look like a loser who couldn't control his own son. Then…"

Shaking her head, she lowered the nibbled cookie to the bare counter, then dusted off her hands.

"Finish, Jewel. And I don't mean the cookie."

Her breath felt like it was scraping her lungs. "When Aaron came in to get his things, Keith did, too. Only as far as the entryway, but when he saw me…he said some pretty nasty things."

"Nasty…how?"

Jewel had already learned, the softer Silas's voice, the tighter rein he was trying to keep on his temper. And this was as soft as she'd ever heard it.

"For one thing, that I'd 'stolen' Aaron from him when Keith and my mother were married, and that damned if he was gonna let it happen again. Then he said…" Her eyes filled; she refused to let them spill over. "That we can't talk to each other anymore."

Her brows flew up when Silas let out a laugh. "And exactly how does Keith think he's going to enforce that? Unless he somehow makes sure the kid never has access to a phone or computer ever again—"

"Silas, you don't understand…" Jewel swallowed down the bile trying to rise in her throat. "Keith accused me of… of having an inappropriate relationship with his son."

Never in her life had she seen a man look more shocked. And then, more furious. "When you were *children?*"

"Yeah."

"Because, what? He'd crawl into bed with you when he was scared? That's demented, Jewel. That he would even think that, I mean. You…" He gave his head a hard shake like he was trying to dislodge the words from his skull, before meeting her gaze again. "It's a damn good thing I wasn't here, or I would've knocked the creep clear into next week. You would *never* hurt a child! Or anybody else, for that matter."

Jewel felt something inside her stretch. Hard. To the point of hurting. "Thank you, but…isn't that a leap of faith? I mean, you don't really know me."

His gaze seared hers. "I know enough," he said quietly, then banged his hand on the counter. "For God's sake—does the man have a screw loose? Did you tell him Aaron didn't even stay here last night?"

"Aaron did himself. Keith didn't believe him. Or chose not to. But he said if I knew what was good for me I'd never contact Aaron again."

One side of Silas's mouth pulled up. "And if he's so all-fired convinced you're some kind of monster, why hasn't he said something before?"

Jewel felt her forehead pinch. "Because he has no proof?"

"Exactly. There's no there, there, honey. And unless Aaron corroborates his father's accusations—"

"True or not, if Keith made a stink it could cost me my career." Jewel picked up her cookie, took a tiny bite, put it down again. No solace in still-warm chocolate chips this time. "I'm only grateful it didn't last long. Tad—"

"Will be fine." The gentleness in Silas's voice nearly did her in. "He's a Garrett, remember? And anyway, it wasn't your fault."

"Maybe not, but I've already been accused of screwing up one kid. Don't need any more traumas on my conscience, thank you."

A moment or two slipped by before Silas went to the fridge for a carton of milk. He held it up, offering; when she nodded, he pulled two glasses out of the cupboard, poured milk into both, then handed her one. "I'm guessing," he said carefully as he returned to his seat, "you didn't see that side of Keith before?"

Yeah, there was that. Jewel took a bigger bite of cookie, washing it down with three large swallows of milk. At Silas's slight smile, she frowned. He pointed to her mouth. "Mustache."

"Oh." She grabbed the same wet towel from before and cleaned herself up, grateful for the break in the conversation to collect her thoughts. Not to mention tell her fluttering stomach to shut the bleep up.

"Didn't see it, or didn't want to?" she said at last, then shrugged. "He wasn't around all that much. But when he was…" The glass set on the counter, she skated her finger around and around the rim. "He was someone else for my mother to lean on instead of me. So I convinced myself I loved him. Only now…" She let out a pitiful little laugh. "Now I'm wondering if I'd confused love with gratitude. And if I was…then I guess I was living in as much of a dream world as my mother."

"Oh, honey…" Silas walked over and pulled her close. And damned if she didn't settle right in like she belonged there, even if this was only a big brother kind of hug.

Which was probably why she totally didn't see the kiss coming. At all. Seriously, when Silas pulled back and smiled down at her she figured that's all it was going to be. A smile.

Um, no.

And, my, oh, my, did the man kiss like he knew what kissing was supposed to be all about, slow and sweet and tender, his hands carefully cradling her jaw, his lips incredibly soft. Firm. Perfect. And anybody who says that slow and sweet and tender can't get a girl's jets going needs their head examined, because Jewel was here to tell anybody who cared to listen that after thirty seconds she was ready to rip her clothes off. Or his, didn't matter.

Except, of course, everybody's clothes stayed put because there were problems to solve and kids to be fetched and whatnot, so Silas let her go, returning to the plate of cookies with his glass of milk—

Hol-y mackerel.

"Um…Silas…?"

He put up one hand, looking a little sheepish. "Don't ask. Because I couldn't give you a coherent answer if I tried."

Well, that explains a lot. Not.

"You can't seriously be attracted to me?"

His brows dipped. "You did not just say that."

"Didn't want to *assume*."

For a split second a smile played around his mouth. Then he said, "Did I offend you?"

"What? No—!"

"Good. Because I could've sworn you kissed me back."

"You caught me off guard, I didn't have any choice."

"So…I did offend you."

"You *surprised* me, Silas. I kissed you back because you're a good kisser, and it was—" *incredible* "—nice, and it's been a long time since—" *anybody gave a damn* "—I locked lips with anybody, either. But—" she huffed out a breath "—but it was weird."

"Weird?"

"Not icky weird, just…you-and-me weird. Not to mention situation…ally weird. I mean, really. Right?"

Please agree, please agree, please agree, she inwardly begged, as the full impact of her reaction to that one little kiss whomped her upside the head, shoving her even closer to the same danged trap that'd snagged her mother umpteen million times.

Because you know what? Right now it was real tempting to let Silas take over, to walk back into that warm, solid embrace and never come out again. To not only let him take care of her, but—and here was the trap part—believe that it would actually last. Except, how many times had that little scenario worked for her mother? That's right—exactly zero. So what was the freaking point?

Fortunately, while she was trying to figure out a way to word this without sounding like a total nitwit, Silas quietly said, "Don't read more into it than what it was. It was just…one of those impulse things. Forget it ever happened, okay?"

It took Jewel a second or two to identify the odd, sharp pain in her midsection as letdown. When, you know, it should have been relief? "Of course!" she said, her eagerness sounding hideously lame even to her own ears. "Impulse, got it." She gave him a thumb's up, then shoved her hands into her back pockets. "Friends?"

Silas gave her a curious look, then smiled. "Sure," and Jewel grabbed the opportunity to swing the conversation back to a topic guaranteed to wipe the kiss from both their minds.

"For what it's worth, after what happened today I understand more than ever how you feel about the boys. I can't imagine how awful it must've been having their mom die in that car crash."

Silas's gaze stroked hers for a long moment, before, his cookie finished, he brushed off his hands, then fisted his hand over his mouth before clearing his throat, as though weighing whether or not to say what he was thinking. "No, what was awful was having no earthly idea where they were for a solid week before that."

Jewel's stomach turned. "What?"

Silas met her gaze. "I had primary custody. Amy had

them every other weekend." He removed his glasses to rub his eyelids, looking ten years older when he put them back on. "Except one Sunday she didn't bring them back."

"Oh, God, Silas…what a nightmare."

"Yeah," he said flatly, then rubbed his palm along his jaw before folding his arms across his chest. "And since she was their mother the local police didn't seem to take it seriously. Far as they were concerned I was *overreacting,* that when she got tired of going it alone—or needed money—she'd show up, I should just sit tight."

"That's outrageous. She'd kidnapped them!"

Another tight smile stretched across his face. "And yet, *I* was overreacting. Go figure." He sighed. "Then about a week later, sheriff calls me. Amy'd skidded on some ice on a back road outside Farmington, slammed into a cement guard rail. She wasn't wearing her seat belt. Thank God the boys were."

It took a moment. "They…the babies were in the car *with* her?"

"Yeah."

On a soft moan, Jewel went to him, threading her arms around his ribs from behind and laying her cheek against his back. His heart beating steadily, reassuringly against her ear, he laid his hand over both of hers. And yeah, she knew she was slipping right back into dangerous territory, but them's the breaks.

"The boys…" His back expanded with his breath. "They'll always come first."

Jewel released him, moving around to see his face, wanting so bad to cup her hands around that face, smooth away those worry lines, she could hardly stand it. Instead, she curled her fingers around his and squeezed.

"Of course they will," she said softly, looking into those

sweet, steady eyes and feeling scarily like Alice tumbling down the rabbit hole. "Thank you for telling me."

Nodding, he slid off the stool. "Guess I better go rescue them, huh?"

"Yeah," she said, watching him go, thanking her lucky stars she'd had the good sense not to mistake rogue kisses and longing glances for something more than they were, because it was perfectly obvious Silas was no more in the market for a new Mrs. Garrett than he had been before. So, good news—she could tumble down that rabbit hole from now 'til Doomsday but she'd never hit bottom…because Silas wasn't gonna let her.

Yes, indeedy, no worries there.

Yay.

Chapter Ten

"You *told* her?" Noah said, setting another bundle of shingles on the conveyer belt to haul them onto Eli's roof, where the laughing, gabbing crew were divvying them out. "For two years," he huffed, bending over to heft the next case, "you've refused to talk about what really happened." The shingles thumped onto the belt; he reached for the next batch. "Never mind the hell we *all* went through when we realized Amy'd basically stolen the kids."

At the disconcerting blend of curiosity and aggravation darkening his brother's eyes, Silas said, "You think I should've kept my mouth shut?"

That got a rough laugh. "Hell, no. About damn time you opened up to somebody about it. No, the question is—" another piercing glare "—why now? Or more specifically, why Jewel?"

For a hundred reasons that would only make sense to Silas. For five hundred more even he couldn't figure out.

However, to admit to his brother that he was falling for the woman, big-time would be the dumbest thing he'd ever done. Strike that: to admit to *Jewel* he was falling for her, *that* would be the dumbest thing he'd ever done. If not the dumbest thing any man in history had ever done.

Granted, when Jewel gave Silas the opening to talk about Amy and the boys a few days ago, all he'd seen—at first—was a way to show her how much he empathized with what she was going through with Aaron. However, reliving the experience had breathed new life into old objections, making him remember why, for so long, he'd been completely uninterested in "getting out there." What was at stake if he did.

And that, in turn, had made him understand all too clearly the fear he'd seen in Jewel's eyes after that kiss.

"Dunno. Maybe because, after what had happened with her brother, I just thought…it would help." His shoulders bumped. "No more to it than that. So…house will be all done by Monday, you said?"

"That's the plan," Noah said after a telling pause, then gave Silas one of his no-good grins. "Because I know you cannot wait to get the woman out of your hair, right?"

Homeboy had no idea.

Hunched against the sudden stiff breeze rustling the last-gasp leaves, Silas walked back to his Explorer feeling as if he was trying to navigate a tiny sailboat in the middle of a raging typhoon at sea—desperately fighting to stay upright, to fend off the emotional storm raging inside him, around him, while Jewel was waaaay off on the shore, thanking her lucky stars she wasn't in the boat.

Oh, sure, she'd responded to that what-*was*-he-thinking? kiss. And quite nicely, too. No surprise there, considering her whole living-life-to-the-fullest bent. But she'd made it patently clear she wasn't looking for forever, and why, and

Silas wasn't so much of a fool as to think one kiss was going to magically undo a lifetime of insecurities. Unfortunately, that *this* woman should be the one to get to him in ways nobody else had been able to—okay, to be fair, what he hadn't allowed anybody else to do—was the *Why, God?* part of things. But her not knowing what she had, what she *was*, her blindness to her own strengths, just made him want to…to…

He sighed: to take care of her. The one thing she'd made plain she didn't want, because that was the one thing she didn't, or couldn't, trust. Not that she didn't deserve being done for the way she'd apparently done for others since she was a child. Nor was Silas defining "taking care" in terms of protecting her. Grown women didn't need protecting. But they did need, and had a right, to be supported. Cherished. Given the space and opportunity to be who and what they needed to be.

So the irony was that space was the one thing, if not the only thing, he could give her that wouldn't freak her out. Which left him no choice but to step aside and let her get on with it.

Even if it killed him.

"So," Noah said through Jewel's cell phone as she navigated Winnie Black's steep driveway through a bobbing cloud of chickens, "house will be all finished by this afternoon. You can move back anytime."

She stopped, idly petting Annabelle, who'd sauntered over to herd her the rest of the way up the hill. A frigid mountain breeze teased the lightweight scarf loosely draped over her short jacket, her thighs through her dark tights. Maybe the denim miniskirt hadn't been such a bright idea. "Wow. Already?"

Noah chuckled. "I would've figured that news would

have you jumping for joy. I *lived* with my brother, remember. Biggest pain in the butt in four states."

"Oh, he's not that bad," Jewel said, her seventy percent off cowboy boots loudly clunking against the already weathered wood when she reached the porch.

"Yeah, well, I'm guessing he doesn't torment you like he did us."

Wouldn't be too sure about that, Jewel thought, finally ringing the doorbell. "Well. Thanks. It will be good to sleep in my own bed again," she said, but her heart wasn't really in it.

But then, what did her heart know?

"Hey. Everything all right?"

A good guy, that Noah. And a good friend, despite his player rep. Donna and Gene Garrett had done a knockout job with all their boys. She briefly thought of Aaron, who'd sent her a miserable, clandestine e-mail on his school computer that morning, pointlessly wishing—

"Enough," Jewel said, hugging one arm to her stomach and shivering. "Worrying about my brother, though."

"Yeah, Si told me about Aaron. That sucks. How's he getting on?"

She sighed. "Not well. His step-mom-to-be's not exactly his best friend, and his father…" Another shiver tracked up her spine. "Just not a good situation all 'round. And the worst of it is…I can't even send him cookies or anything because I'm not supposed to be communicating with him!"

"So give our mom his address, let her send cookies. There's ways around this crap, Jewel. Always."

"I know, but…it would be nice not to have to sneak, like we're outlaws or something."

"Si said you're really worried about him."

Jewel twisted back around, facing the view of the valley sweeping away from the porch, an impressionistic blur of dusty golds and browns and greens through her waterlogged eyes. Si said this, Si said that…every day, he asked about Aaron, his genuine concern shredding her heart, her common sense. Her resolve. Thank God she'd be out of the house soon, before she did something stupid.

More stupid, anyway.

"Worried sick," she finally said. "He got such a raw deal, Noah, it breaks my heart…oh, here's Winnie. Catch you later."

For the next half hour, Jewel somehow managed to immerse herself in the only part of her life that wasn't making her loopy, after which Winnie insisted on giving her a cup of tea in the Blacks' large, homey kitchen while Robbie let Seamus climb all over him in the nearby den and tiny Aisling slept peacefully in her swing, oblivious to all the goings-on.

"First off," Winnie said, sliding a check across the table along with a cup of English breakfast tea, "we wanted to give you this."

Jewel glanced at the check for half Patrice's fee, only to frown when she noticed Winnie had made it out to Jewel by mistake. She handed it back. "I'm guessing you're not getting a whole lot of sleep, you need to make this out to Patrice, not me."

"Already paid Patrice," Winnie said, easing herself into the chair opposite, her long fingers cradling her own cup of tea. "That's for you. And not one word from you, Miss Thing. We can afford it and I know how little you gals make. Besides, you deserve it. We gave Patty a hefty tip, too, if that puts your mind at ease."

Blinking, Jewel stared at the check. "I don't know what to say."

"How about 'thank you'?" Winnie said, and Jewel nearly spewed tea through her nose. Then she got up to give Winnie a big hug, before sitting again and picking up her purse off the floor beside her chair, glancing at the check one last time before tucking it inside.

"Thank you. And bless you. Now that Eli's house is fixed up, I suppose he'll be wanting to sell it. So the money'll help me get a place of my own...."

And why on earth that should get her all down in the dumps, Jewel had no idea. Especially since she should be over the moon about the unexpected windfall....

"Okay, what's up, cutie?" Winnie said, bringing Jewel's eyes to her bright blue ones. "You are definitely not your normal, perky self. Or is sleep deprivation making me hallucinate?"

Since Jewel thought of Winnie more as a friend than a client, it wasn't as if she took offense at the woman's prying. But her emotions about Aaron and Silas and, well, all of it were so close to the surface. And the last thing she wanted was to sound like She Who Must Not Be Emulated.

So she smiled and said, "It's nothing" before the pity demons could get a foothold, and then the baby woke up squawking for her lunch and Jewel mumbled something about having another appointment anyway, which was a big fat lie but a chicken's gotta do what a chicken's gotta do. *Bawk, bawk.*

So she got outta there by the hair of her chinny-chin-chin—or feathers, whatever—even though she was still kinda shaky when she ducked into the town's tiny supermarket to pick up something to cook for dinner. Where she neatly dodged Silas's sister-in-law Tess with her two kids and pregnant glow, partly because all this happiness stuff was wearing on a person, partly because Winnie and Tess were best buds and she could hear the conversation now:

"Got any idea what's up with Jewel?"

"Not really, but I've got my theories..."

Because in a small town people always had theories, even if they were based on air. Then Tess would say something to Eli, probably, who'd undoubtedly blab everything to Silas, since the four brothers were tight as ticks.

So, the *bawk-bawk-bawking* about to split her head in two, Jewel grabbed some pork chops and elbow macaroni, swiped her card through the self-serve dealie and got the heck out of there, picked up Ollie from school and Tad from Mrs. Maple's, grateful the day was warm enough to send them out back to play in the tree house. Not because she didn't want them underfoot, but because Ollie had rushed into her arms when she came to get him, reminding her so much of Aaron when she used to pick him up from school she ached.

Except no sooner had she plunked the pork chops into a casserole dish with a mess of stuff she found in the pantry than the weather did a one-eighty, a sharp wind blowing in a herd of ugly, angry clouds to smother the sun and sending a pair of panting, shivering little boys back inside.

"S'cold," Tad said, diving for the sofa and wrapping his arms around a snoring, comatose Doughboy, who didn't even flinch.

"C'n we have hot chocolate?" Ollie said, only to roll his eyes practically up underneath his bangs when Jewel raised her brows at him. "*May* we have hot chocolate?"

"Only half a cup, 'cause it's too close to dinner—"

"Daddy!" the boys yelled in unison, rushing him, and the dog slid off the sofa with an ungainly thump and wriggle-waddled over to join the joyous reunion, and Silas—his arms full of smelly children and even smellier dog—lifted his eyes to Jewel's and smiled, all honey-I'm-home and whatnot…and the goodness and loneliness and not-even-gonna-try-to-hide-it desire she saw there flat out stole her breath, making her ache all the more. And in a way totally inappropriate with children in the room.

Jewel was stronger than the ache. She knew that. Knew, too, she could resist the reciprocal longing in Silas's eyes. Knew it, because she'd done it before, when opportunity alone hadn't seemed like a good enough reason to get naked with somebody.

Except the longer he held her gaze, the sweeter and hotter his became and the louder the little imp in her head sniggered, urging her to...to...

Do something for herself, for once.

Not that anybody said anything—couldn't, anyway, with kids in the room. But she guessed Silas was thinking the same thing, that after two years of putting the boys first he yearned to do something for himself, too.

Oh, this was bad. Very, very bad.

Especially when he peeled off kids and pooch and said, "Go play, okay?" and they did and he came into the kitchen, leaned against the counter and quietly said, "What's wrong?" Except not in that irritated tone of voice most people did when what they really meant was "Would you please get over whatever this is so things can get back to normal?" but as if he honest to God wanted to make it better. Or at least try.

Not that she was about to confess about all the aching, no sirree. Pride and all that. And in any case the moment he asked she realized the crazies in her head had as much to do with her stepbrother as they did Silas. That, she could talk about.

So she told him about the stealth e-mail, then said, "Oh, God, Silas—he's so unhappy it breaks my heart. Keith won't let him hang with his friends at all, or even get rides home with them from school. Then when he's home, he's pretty much confined to his room because he and his dad's fiancée don't get along at all, but Keith disabled his wireless access on his computer so he can't even talk to his friends online. He has his phone, but Keith is keeping real close tabs on all his calls and texts. It's horrible," she pushed past the lump in her throat. "He's acting like, like a prison guard, not a father! And I'm not supposed to be crying!"

"Says who?" Silas said, folding her into his arms, resting his chin atop her head. "Because you think it's a sign of weakness?" When she nodded against his shirt, he chuckled. "Bull. My mom's one of the toughest gals I know, she cries at the drop of a hat. So you go right ahead and let it out, not gonna bother me—"

"Why's Jewel crying?" she heard Ollie ask, worried. But when she tried to pull away, Silas held fast.

"She's just having a sad," Silas said over her head, and then both little boys wrapped their arms around her legs and hugged her, too. Tad even patted her butt—since he couldn't really reach her back—and told her it would be okay, making her softly laugh…making her yearn for far more than…the other thing.

So it was with profound relief that, right before she served dinner, Patrice called—Abby Iglesias's water had broken ten days early. With any luck, she thought as she kissed the boys goodnight, assiduously avoiding eye contact with their father, it would be hours and hours before the baby came and Silas would have been asleep for hours and hours by the time she got back.

Except, when she let her still-andrenalized self into the house sometime after two in the morning, the flickering light from the TV pulled her into the living room. His hands laced behind his head, Silas sat on the sofa in his robe and PJ bottoms, watching a movie. Despite the chill in the house, the robe gapped on top, partially exposing his chest and provoking that weird craving-something-but-no-idea-what feeling in the center of Jewel's.

Except she knew darn well *what*.

In theory, she could have returned to Eli's. In fact, if she hadn't gone out on that delivery, she would've probably hauled her stuff back there tonight. But she had, so she hadn't, so here she was.

Having cravings.

"Couldn't sleep?" she whispered, a small shiver tracking up her spine.

Still focused on the screen, Silas shrugged. "Apparently not."

"Want anything?"

Finally, his eyes shifted to hers. "You have no idea."

The shiver turned to a rush of hoo-*Mama* heat over her face, her chest. "I take it we're not talking hot chocolate and toast."

His gaze locked in hers, he shook his head, then released a soft, self-deprecating laugh. "And you probably are."

She took a deep breath, then another, knowing the next move was hers. That Silas was far too much of a gentleman to come right out and ask. "Just so you know? I'm on the Pill."

Loooong silence. "You sure?"

"That I'm on the Pill—?"

"No," Silas said with another laugh. "About wanting—"

"To sleep with you? Yes."

His head angled slightly, his gaze so steady she half wondered if she'd misread him. "Why?"

"Because I think…it would be…fun." *And because it might be nice to do this with somebody I actually liked, for a change.*

"Yeah," he said softly. "Me, too. Unless…you're too tired…?"

Ohmi-freaking-gosh. This was really happening.

"Are you kidding? I got to catch another baby, I'm so wired I could send signals to Mars."

"Okay." Then he smiled. "So…wanna make out?"

Jewel clamped her hand over her mouth to smother her laugh, lowering it to whisper, "What is this, high school?"

"Except I never made out in high school."

"Seriously? *Never?*"

"If you'd seen me in high school, you'd understand."

"That's so sad," she said, and he chuckled, all low and sexy and full of promise; and then she said, "you know, if you'd chuckled like that back then, you'd've had to fight 'em off with sticks," and he laughed again and patted the space beside him.

"Come here," he murmured, setting his glasses on the end table, and she went thinking…she could handle this, right?

And the imp's sniggers morphed into full-out guffaws.

Ignoring it—them, whatever—Jewel ditched her own glasses, her boots, her qualms, sinking into the deep cushions with a sigh when Silas eased her back into the sofa, shielding her with all that steady, quiet strength as their mouths met in a kiss that was serious flame-to-pilot-light time. *Whoosh.*

Almost startled, she pulled back only to realize his crooked, barely visible smile in the dim light, the *Hah!* look in his eyes was far more dangerous than his mouth.

Or so she told herself as she skimmed her fingers through his hair and kissed him again.

* * *

What was that old saying? If this was wrong, he didn't want to be right?

It'd been a long, long time since Silas had fooled around with his babies asleep right down the hall, since he'd experienced the skin-tingling thrill of heightened awareness that went with it. Since he'd fooled around, period. But, cloaked in the near-darkness as each lingering, lazy kiss melted into the next, the initial prickles of anxiety also melted, into I-can-die-happy-now anticipation.

Until the sudden pressure of Jewel's hands on his shoulders brought his head up to see the same old ghosts of ambivalence in her eyes. Brushing her hair off her cheek, he smiled, even if it was probably a little shaky. "Change your mind?"

"And wouldn't you be one miserable dude if I had?"

Wrapping one arm around her waist, Silas shifted them on the cushions to put some breathing space between her thigh and his erection. "I'd survive."

Now on her side, Jewel carefully wedged her elbow between Silas and the back of the couch to prop her head in her hand. "I'm not backing out, Si. Promise. But…you do know this is a one-off, right?"

Of course he knew that. Had known from the moment, hours before, when their eyes locked in the kitchen and *want* bounced back and forth between them like a flubberized Ping-Pong ball. Which is why he kicked disappointment right out on its sorry butt.

"I kinda figured. Hey…" He stroked his thumb across her cheek. "Is that what's bothering you? That you think I'm expecting more from you than you're ready to give?" When, after a moment, she nodded, he slipped his hand underneath her now loose hair, kissed her lightly on the mouth and tugged her down to cuddle, ignoring disappointment over there in the corner making faces at him. "Then maybe you should stop thinking so much," he said softly, "and simply enjoy the moment. Because I certainly intend to."

Hesitantly, she traced one finger across his pecs. "You're really okay with that?"

He pushed out a short, dry laugh. "I haven't had sex in more than two years. What do you think?"

"Get out!" She wriggled free to prop herself up again. "Two *years?*"

"Nice to know you've been swapping spit with the biggest freak on the planet, right?"

"Actually…it's kind of sweet. In a freaky kind of way." She settled in again. "Any particular reason?"

Silas paused, weighing his answer. "Didn't even think about it that much, to be truthful. Okay, I *thought* about it," he said when she chuckled. "But I wasn't motivated to do anything more than that." His fingers drifted up and down her arm. "Until a little bit ago."

When the scales fell from my eyes.

"But hey," she said. "No pressure."

"None at all. Honey…I really do understand that things are up in the air for you right now. So I'm okay about this being whatever you want it to be, as long as you're up-front with me about that. Only thing that'll make me mad is if you say or do something because you think that's what I *want* you to say or do."

She frowned. "I'd never do that. Especially to you. I'm not even sure I'm capable of it."

"I know you're not." In fact, her honesty was probably the main reason they were here right now. Issues, she had, but game-playing wasn't one of them. Sexiest thing ever.

Never mind that he was doing the very thing he'd made her promise not to do—saying what he knew she needed to hear. To a certain extent, anyway. Because he *didn't* want her to feel she had to pretend with him, or feel pressured into something she wasn't ready for. The point was to make her feel safe, that she could trust him. And how could he do that if he told her how he really felt?

Just your average, everyday moral dilemma, yep.

"So," she said. "What now?"

"So…we could keep making out and make ourselves crazy, stop making out and make ourselves crazier…or move things into my bedroom—which has an actual lock on the door—and get as crazy as we want."

She paused. "Thought you didn't do crazy."

"Yeah, surprised the hell out of me, too," he said, then stood and hauled her into his arms in one surprisingly smooth motion, considering how long it'd been since he'd attempted such a thing, and she curled herself around him, completely trusting he wouldn't let her fall.

Even though he was in far more danger of that than she was.

The thing was, Jewel wasn't one of those women who pondered things a great deal during sex. Well, unless it was really bad—you know, the kind where you're wondering *Oh, dear heaven, is this ever going to be over?* or you sort of lose focus and start thinking about all the stuff you have to do the next day. When the sex was good, though, she'd found that more often than not the whole experience was one big rush of sensation and not a lot of point-by-point detail.

Such, however, was not the case this time. Not that sensations weren't rushing and all, but losing focus? Not an option. She should've known, the man was a freaking accountant, details were his *life*.

And now, they were hers.

She'd had no idea her upper arms were erogenous zones.

Or her knees. Or the space between her shoulder blades. Or, that by the time he actually got around to the parts that were *supposed* to be erogenous zones, she'd be a basket case. As in writhing, whimpering and whining, which for some bizarre reason only egged him on. She also wondered—just idly, you understand, the merest passing thought—what on earth was wrong with his ex, to have voluntarily walked away from—

"Oh!" Jewel's head dropped back as Silas cupped her bottom and lowered his mouth—

This.

About that attention to detail thing…uh, yeah. As in, let's take our time, shall we? As in, dude was clearly having every bit as much fun as she was, which was going some since right now there were some major fireworks going off in her brain. Not to mention—

Holy moly, she thought, biting her lip to stifle what would have been the scream to end all screams, as befitted the orgasm to end all orgasms. Lord, she'd be trembling from this one for a week. Then he slipped inside her, and she thought, *Okay, fine, your turn, only fair,* except—

Oh.

Oh, wow. Was this even possible?

Apparently so, since not long after a very nice aftershock in the 5.4 range or so rumbled through, right about the time Silas's Big One struck.

All of which would have struck her funny—well, actually, it did, she burst into a fit of muffled laughter right after—only then Silas's eyes caught hers and panic streaked through her as she realized, *Oh, fudge—you lied!*

Over the imp's reeeeeally loud *Gotcha!* in her head.

It's okay, you can still salvage this, ignore the imp and play it cool—

Right. Except for the small issue of Silas looking so…

happy. And not happy like a man who just scored—well, maybe a little, around the eyes—but *happy,* happy.

As in, in love, happy. Or so Jewel guessed, her experience in such matters being somewhat limited.

Lying on his side, Silas looped an arm around her waist, his face all sappy and grinny and dopey. She couldn't *handle* the sappy/grinny/dopey face. She couldn't.

"That was fun," he whispered, his thumb toying with the underside of one little A-cup breast. A breast which he'd said was the prettiest thing he'd ever seen, right before he proved how much, in this case, size *doesn't* matter. Her nipple tingled, begging. *More, please?*

Right about the same time her heart said pretty much the same thing. Only louder. Because now Silas was the one inviting *her* inside, both offering her sanctuary and laying more than two years' worth of caution on the altar...for *her.*

"Sure was," Jewel said, pushing her mouth into a smile before pushing herself upright. "And ohmigosh, look at the time. We're both gonna be like zombies in the morning—"

She fought her way out of the tangled linens to look for her clothes, realizing this didn't exactly qualify as playing it cool. Behind her, she heard Silas sigh, then get up to yank his pajama bottoms back on.

"You know, if this had been ten years ago," he said quietly, "I would have assumed either one or both of us was having drunken regrets or my skills in the sack were lacking. Since neither of us has been drinking that puts paid to option number one. And since I'm also gonna go out on a limb and guess you weren't faking it, that shoots option number two all to hell, too. So what's wrong?"

Zipping up her skirt, Jewel hmmphed out a laugh. And

ignored his question. "You've never had a drunken regret in your life."

"No, but I've had plenty of sober ones." Out of the corner of her eye, she saw his arms fold across his bare chest. "And I'm sure hoping this isn't one of them. Not for my sake, Jewel—I'm a big boy, I can handle your buyer's remorse. But it appears you can't."

Her arms through her T-shirt, she jerked down the hem. "This isn't buyer's remorse! I knew exactly what I was doing when I went to bed with you!"

"Except that was before and this is now. And judging from the look on your face, I'm guessing now isn't so good, is it?" Obvious consternation twisting his features, he took a step closer. "It was just like you said, honey—two adults, one night of enjoying each other. Nothing more than that—"

"Liar!" she said, keeping her voice low, knowing how easily children could hear the grownups arguing. "That's not all it was for you! Was it?"

He didn't react. Not outwardly, at least. Instead all he did was stand there, his gaze probing. She tore hers away, but not before she saw that knowing, gentle smile curve his mouth.

"Maybe not. But is that really why you're upset right now? Or because…that's not all it was for *you?*"

Heat flooding her face, Jewel rammed her arms into her sweater, muttering, "Noah said the house is ready, I think it's best I go back there tonight. You'll…" Oh, brother. "I don't know when I'll be here tomorrow. Is that a problem?"

Instead of replying, he walked over to take her face in his hands and kiss her. Long. Slow. Sweet. With just enough *You're mine now, baby* in there to make her knees wobble. Because, dammit, she wanted to be his. To be *somebody's.* Even though she knew it was stupid.

"We'll be fine, honey," he said, silently opening the bedroom door for her. "And so will you."

Not so sure about that, she thought, grabbing her boots from the floor and her glasses off the table, her qualms scurrying to catch up with her again as she fled.

Chapter Eleven

Her arms tightly crossed over the raggedy Betty Boop nightshirt she'd left behind when she moved into Silas's, Jewel stared at her cell phone, vibrating on the kitchen table in front of her. She didn't answer it, even though she knew she should. Even though she knew it was Silas—he'd already phoned and texted her a dozen times since 7:00 a.m.—and if she didn't answer he was likely to show up on her doorstep. Because that's the kind of man he was.

The kind of man who made love like it was his mission to make her happy, who had no problem asking exactly what it would take to accomplish that. And then thanking *her* after he did what she asked and her head exploded. Among other things.

The kind of man to make a girl go and fall in love with him, even though she'd made it more than clear *she didn't want to do that.*

Bzzzzt.

She snatched the damn phone off the table, her heart whomping against her sternum as she read the succinct text.

You okay?

Leave it to Silas to actually write both words out, she thought on a sigh, then texted back, *yes. fine. c u later*

An inevitability, alas, since she still had small boys to tend for another few days at least. Drat.

She jumped up to toss on a pair of jeans and a cropped sweater, then stomped into the living room to crash onto the sofa, hauling *Holistic Midwifery*—also left behind—into her lap. Nope, focusing not happening.

Not on midwifery, anyway. Not while every molecule that made up her being was still doing the happy sigh thing. Traitors.

The outside world beckoned. As did Evangelista's homemade cinnamon rolls and a breakfast burrito. Her stomach growling in agreement, Jewel stuffed her feet into her boots and the book into a backpack and practically ran out of the house, embracing the slimmest of slim hopes the two mile trek down the mountain would at least lull all those happy-sighing molecules to sleep.

Right. Like she was gonna walk this off?

Frowning, hands stuffed in jacket pockets, she marched along the side of the road, occasionally blinking against the flashes of sunlight darting through the yellowing trees. Yes, she could've walked away. Could've stayed in control. After all, nobody'd forced her into the man's bed. That things hadn't gone the way she'd deluded herself into thinking they would wasn't anybody's fault but her own.

And maybe—just maybe—that's not such a bad thing?

Jewel stopped dead in her tracks, dust blowing in her face as an old Chevy pickup roared past. So falling for

Silas—for anybody—hadn't been part of her game plan. So what? Was she really that afraid to take the next step, to simply see where things went after this?

And that would be a resounding *You betcha, sister.*

Right there in the middle of the road, Jewel let out a frustrated screech, pounding her forehead with the heels of her hands. Then, feeling marginally better, she continued down the mountain.

"Hey there, baby doll!" Evangelista Ortega called out when Jewel shouldered through the door thirty minutes later. The bosomy proprietress of the only decent restaurant in town—okay, the only restaurant in town—waddled over to engulf Jewel in a hug. "Haven't seen you in a while. How's things going?"

To hell, Jewel thought, even as she said, "Oh. Fine," extricating herself from the woman's embrace before she suffocated. Then she grinned, even if it felt more like a grimace. "I'm delivering babies myself now!"

"Oh, yeah? *Felicitaciónes,* chica! I also hear you've been doing the nanny thing for Silas Garrett, no?"

Yep, definitely a grimace. "Uh, yeah. So. Busy. Um... you mind if I hang out here and study?"

Evangelista gave her a funny look, but jerked her thumb over her shoulder at an empty table all the way in the back. "Jus' cleaned that one up, it's yours. You wan' breakfas'?" she said as Jewel unloaded her backpack and settled in.

"Do I want breakfast? Juice, breakfast burrito and two cinnamon rolls. Oh, and I have money, I can actually pay—"

"Don' *even* go there!" the other woman said with a swat, then laughed. "Although the way you eat? It's probably a good thing you don' come in more often than you do!"

Jewel slouched in the chair, sparing a grin for the young waitress who brought her order, stuffing a chunk of warm

warm, fragrant, gooey cinnamon roll into her mouth before the gal turned her back. Bliss. Fifteen minutes later, her tummy appeased and finally absorbed in the textbook, she'd finally started feeling almost normal again.

Until the restaurant's front door opened and her mother cried out, "There you are, baby!" and she felt like she'd swallowed the fifteen-hundred-page hardcover whole.

The moon, Jewel thought. *Maybe that would be far enough away....*

Bedecked in a flippy skirt, fuzzy sweater and a fake fur vest, Kathryn glided through a dozen tables to plop herself across from Jewel...and thrust a diamond the size of Nebraska in her face.

"I'm in love and I'm gettin' married!" her mother sang out, which earned her a smattering of applause from the other patrons.

Just...no, Jewel thought, stunned. Her mother, signaling for a cup of coffee, appeared not to notice.

"It only happened last night, but I couldn't tell you over the phone. I had to do it in person." Then she snatched her hand back to wriggle it in the sunlight dancing across the table. "Isn't it *gorgeous?*" Kathryn glanced over, glowing more than the diamond. Than the sun, for that matter. "Well, come on, sugar—aren't you going to congratulate me?"

The coffee arrived. "Tell me first who my new daddy is and I'll think about it."

Giggling, her mother tore open a package of fake sugar, upended it. "Why Monty, of course! Who else?"

"Monty. The Monty who broke up with you a few weeks ago?"

Mama batted her hand. The diamond encrusted one, naturally. "Oh, that was just a silly lover's tiff. He's the sweetest man, baby." Holding out her hand again to admire the ring, her mother sighed, then took a delicate sip of her decaf. "The *sweetest* man."

"I wouldn't know," Jewel said dryly, even as the cinnamon rolls and burrito rebelled in her stomach. "Having never met him. Come to think of it, I don't even know his last name."

"James. Montgomery Hamilton James. He's a businessman with a biiiig—" this demonstrated by her mother's stretching out her arms so wide she nearly clipped Christine, the waitress "—ranch in Texas."

Jewel felt a headache coming on. "And exactly how did you meet a Texas businessman-slash-rancher in Albuquerque?"

"Actually we connected online. Through one of those Internet dating sites?"

Jewel opened her mouth only to clamp it shut again, especially since her mother immediately launched into a soliloquy about the whens/wheres/hows of the wedding and how she wanted Jewel to be her maid of honor and how Monty was going to let her redecorate the ranch house... and, oh, he was making her sign a prenup but that was only a formality, but he had to be careful because his last two wives had taken him to the cleaners—

"Whoa, whoa, whoa. *Last* two wives? Out of how many?"

"Um...let's see..."

"You don't *know?*"

She might've screeched that last part.

Kathryn's brow crinkled. Slightly. "Of course I know. But...you're probably not going to take this well—"

"You're probably right. Well?"

"Four."

"You're about to marry a man who's been married *four times before?*"

She definitely screeched that.

"Well, shoot, baby, I've made the trek up the aisle three times myself. What's the big deal?"

And God help her, she means it, Jewel thought, something like rage boiling up from her gut. Because she looked into her mother's glittering, lovestruck eyes and saw the same delusional soul behind them that had made Jewel's childhood about as stable as a skateboard on ice. Granted, when this marriage crashed and burned like all the others at least it wouldn't affect Jewel, except it would because she'd be the one left to pick up the pieces of her mother's shattered heart. Again.

"And what on earth makes you think this time will work when it never has before?" she said, slamming shut her book and cramming it back into her backpack.

"Jewel! Why would you say that? Everybody needs hope, sugar—"

"No, what you need is *some* grip on reality! Taking a leap of faith is one thing, but you'd think by now you'd at least open your eyes before you jump!"

Instead of getting mad—which even Jewel admitted her mother had every right to do, she was truly talking smack to the woman—Kathryn pouted. "You don't think I know what I'm doing?" she asked in a small voice.

"No, Mama. I don't." And Jewel realized, in this respect at least, she had a leg up on her mother. That she did know enough to open her eyes, to not take a leap without having at least some idea where, and how, to land.

Meaning, no—she couldn't move forward with Silas, no matter how besotted she was with him. How much thinking about him made her all warm and tingly inside. Because it wasn't fair to him, or to his boys, to be saddled with some clueless little twit who still had no idea how to make a relationship work.

Shaking, she got to her feet only to have her mother grab her wrist.

"I want your blessing, baby," Kathryn said, pleading, her nails biting into Jewel's skin.

"You don't need it, Mama. What you need…oh, never mind," she muttered, turning, only to wheel back, her brain finally releasing the question her mother's surprise announcement had temporarily obliterated. "How did you find me here, anyway?"

Kathryn lowered her eyes to her purse to pull out a couple of dollars for her coffee. "Does it matter?"

"Yeah. Because it's creepy, the way you keep popping up. My car's not out front, you had no way of knowing I was in here…oh, hell," Jewel said, her stomach turning inside out. "You had a tracking application installed on the phone you gave me, didn't you? Because that's how Keith found Aaron, through some GPS thing on his phone—"

"Keith? Aaron? What are you talking about—"

"For heaven's sake, Mama!" Her face on fire, Jewel fumbled to get her phone out of her purse. "I'm not some wayward teenager you need to keep tabs on!"

"What else was I supposed to do?" her mother whined. "I have to know where you are in case I need you!"

Jewel stared into her mother's genuinely terrified eyes for several seconds before taking her hand and pressing the phone into it. "You have Monty now, you don't need me," she said, then turned and walked away before her mother could see her tears.

"Sorry, didn't mean to be *this* late." Obviously frazzled, Jewel brushed past Silas on her way into the kitchen. "I had to run into Santa Fe to get a new phone. The boys aren't here?"

"At my folks'. Mom said she needed a grandbaby fix

before she lost her mind. What happened to your old phone?"

He watched as she shucked her backpack onto the kitchen table, shoving her sweater sleeves up to her elbows. "Mama's getting married again," she said, grabbing a bowl of cookie dough she'd made the day before out of the fridge.

"And...there's a correlation between those two things?"

"Yes."

Thinking, *To hell with this,* Silas walked over and gently grasped her shoulders, turning her around. "Hey," he said softly. "Spill."

Conflict screamed in her eyes before, shaking her head, she pulled away. Her back to him, she clanged cookie sheets onto the counter, washed her hands, then began plucking chunks of dough out of the bowl and jerkily rolling them into balls. Then she stopped, gripping the edges of the counter, her shoulders up near her ears.

"Turns out she put this tracking thing on my phone, that's how she always knew where to find me. So she did, at Ortega's. Came in, announced her engagement to some man she found on the Internet, who she's known for God only knows how long—or not—who I've never even met. Oh, and she'll be his fifth wife."

"Ouch."

"Yeah." She smacked the first glob of dough onto the sheet, smashing it down with the bottom of a glass like she was killing a bug. And oh, did Silas know where this was headed.

"Honey—"

"Don't, Si," she whispered. "Please."

Like hell. Again, he curled his hands around her

arms, angled her to face him. "You're not your mother, Jewel—"

"She asked for my blessing, Silas! My approval for something…" Her mouth thinned, she once more put space between them. "I know I'm not my mother. Which is precisely why I refuse to follow in her footsteps."

Yeah, no surprise there. Then why did he feel like he'd just been eviscerated? "I know you need time—"

"And what's going to change a month from now?" she said, wheeling on him, her expression anguished. "A year? Ten years? I see that hope in her eyes, that…that belief she clings to so fiercely that *this* time won't be like the others. No, don't interrupt, I've got to say this."

Her breathing ragged, she knuckled the space between her brows, getting cookie dough all over her glasses. On a strangled groan, she yanked them off and tossed them on the counter, where they skittered away like a scolded puppy. "I look in her eyes," she said in a small voice, tears flooding hers, "and I see…oh, hell."

Glancing at the ceiling, she let out a humorless chuckle, then faced him again. "I see exactly how loving you makes *me* feel," she said, and Silas's heart stopped. "Amazed, and awestruck, and most of all, hopeful. Except, how on earth can I trust any of that? How…" She swallowed, then swiped away a tear. "How can I trust what I see in *your* eyes?"

And here's where being good at something besides numbers might've come in handy, because when far too many seconds passed without Silas answering, Jewel gave another unhappy snort and returned to her chore. "Yeah. That's what I thought."

Helplessness trampled Silas like a bull elephant—a sensation he'd hoped never in his life to feel again. Just like with Amy, he had no earthly idea how to give her what she needed. In Jewel's case, how to staunch the loneliness she'd clearly determined would be her companion to the grave.

"You love me?"

"Yeah," she said, obviously confused. Even more obviously in agony. "Go figure."

Funny, how he couldn't remember Amy ever saying she loved him, although she must have at some point. Early on, though. Before things got hard. Before she realized that loving *was* hard, sometimes. Jewel, though…she already understood that. What she didn't understand yet was that *hard* didn't mean *impossible*.

But only if both people were willing to work at it. Like his parents did, every day of their lives.

"I'd never hurt you, Jewel. You've got to believe that."

Several beats ticked by before she turned again, tears bulging over her lower lashes. "And God knows I *want* to believe you. Want to trust what *I* feel. It's like you opened the door for me, and ohmigosh do I like what I see on the other side, but…"

Two tears broke free to streak down her face. "I'm so sorry, Silas," she whispered. "My problem to work out, sure, but 'maybe' isn't fair to you, or the boys."

His own eyes burning, Silas closed the space between them and drew her close, inhaling her scent, brown sugar and vanilla and flowers-in-a-bottle, and for maybe a half minute he held on tight, wishing desperately for a few magic words that would make her change her mind. But what could he say? That he *needed* her?

As if she'd heard him she jerked away, snatching her glasses off the counter.

"Honey…I'm more than willing to take a chance on this—"

"Yeah, well, I'm not. I *can't*." She shoved her glasses back on, her hair falling in slippery little furrows around her face. "If you don't mind, I think…I'll just finish up these cookies for you and then…take my stuff back to Eli's."

He could barely breathe. "If that's what you want—"

"Although if it's okay with you…I think I'll leave the Beanie Babies for the boys?"

"Oh, uh, sure. But…won't you miss them?"

She almost smiled. "No. Oh! But do you need me to make dinner—?"

"Got it covered," Silas said, even though he didn't. "Well. I guess I'll go get the boys out of Mom's hair." He cleared his throat. "Will you be here when we get back?"

"It'll take me twenty minutes, tops, to toss everything in my car," she said, her back to him as she slid first one, then the other sheet into the oven. "So, no."

With that, Silas was out of words. Or reasons to linger. So he whistled to Doughboy, who'd slept through the whole exchange, and went out to his car, heaving the beast onto the passenger seat and distractedly taking a Handi Wipe to his drool.

"Why am I so lousy at this?" he asked the dog, who gave him a messy schlurp across his chin. Banishing the dog spit with his sleeve, Silas sighed. "I'm really, really gonna miss her, boy."

With a cross between a whine and a groan, Doughboy plopped his head on Silas's knee and rolled his big, brown bloodshot eyes up at him, the picture of commiseration.

The horn honk nearly made Jewel drop the twenty-pound pumpkin she'd just lugged to the other side of Eli's porch. Shielding her eyes from the October sun's last blast of the day, she turned to see, past the For Sale sign at the end of the drive, Noah waving at her from inside that Bad Bart truck of his.

Since she'd left Silas's two weeks before she hadn't run into any of the brothers, despite the house being right next to the family's shop. Seeing Noah now stirred up the heartache all over again. Heartache of her own making, granted, but still. Cutting off something to avoid pain down the road didn't mean it wasn't still going to hurt like holy heck now.

Jewel waved back, fully expecting Noah to drive on. When he didn't, she reluctantly made her way down the porch steps and out to his truck, clutching her jacket closed against the wind.

"Hey," she said to his sassy grin. Dude was definitely cute, no doubt about it. Even though her hormones were all, *Meh, can't be bothered.*

"Hey," he said, the breeze messing with his light brown hair through the open window. "Whatcha been up to?"

Jewel shrugged. "Nothin' much. Packing. Studying. Measuring pregnant bellies. The usual. You?"

He nodded toward the sign. With the big old Sold sticker slapped across it. "You find a place yet?"

"Sorta. The Blacks are going to Ireland for the month. Winnie asked me to dog/chicken/house sit. Buys me a little more time to decide what comes next."

"You're staying in Tierra Rosa, though, right?"

Jewel forced a smile. "We'll see."

Noah looked away, tapping the steering wheel with his thumb. "You gonna ask me about my brother?"

"Sure thing. How's Eli getting on?" His gaze swung to hers and she sighed. "It's a small town, Noah. If anything was going on with Silas or the boys, I'm sure I'd find out." Her eyes narrowed. "Or did he send you to spy on *me*?"

"You kidding? He'd have kittens if he knew I was here."

Jewel shoved her hands in her pockets. "Then why *are* you here?"

"I can't swing by to see how you're doing?"

Out of nowhere, the loneliness swamped her. That she'd lose her mind if she spent one more night with nothing to keep her company but her textbooks and her packing boxes and reruns of *The Gilmore Girls*.

"You got plans for tonight?" she asked.

"Nnnnno," Noah said, suspicion flashing in his eyes. "Why?"

"Hold on," she said, then ran back into the house, grabbed her purse and streaked back out before she could change her mind. The look on Noah's face when she yanked open the passenger door and climbed in was priceless.

"While you're swinging," she said, "how about swinging me out to dinner?"

"You sure that's a good idea?"

"Since I'm starving I think it's an excellent idea."

Noah seemed to ponder this for several seconds before giving the car some gas and steering one-handed away from the curb. "Where'd you like to go?"

"How about the Lone Star? I've never been."

"You're kidding?"

"I know, huh? I've been here almost two years, too."

"No, I mean…" He chuckled. "I don't generally connect the Lone Star and 'dinner' in my head, that's all. Not that there's anything wrong with it, exactly, but…people don't go there for the food. I mean, really, I can spring for dinner someplace where the food isn't served on greasy paper in a plastic basket."

"I'm not asking you to *spring* for anything. I just…I just want company tonight, okay?"

Beside her, Noah stilled. "You might want to define that."

Jewel started to laugh, only to realize exactly how close she was to crying. Shoot. "All I'm asking for is somebody to talk to while I eat my greasy burger and fries." She looked over. "You good with that?"

"What I am, is relieved as hell. Well, okay, then—you got your heart set on the Lone Star, far be it from me to deny you. But you've been warned."

It took barely five minutes, if that, to get to the bar, situated in what used to be an old house not far from the center of town. It was what it was—kitschy and seedy and rundown—and she loved it from the moment the blinking neon glow embraced the truck as they pulled into the rutted parking lot.

Inside was even better, smelling like grease and booze and every hairstyling product known to humankind, and the space seemed to pulse with indistinguishable country music and people all trying to talk over it, and at least a dozen people called out their "Heys" to Noah—and more than one woman, Jewel noticed, gave her a "Who the heck are you?" once-over that she found strangely gratifying, and she thought, *Yes, perfect.*

"Bar or table?" Noah shouted in her ear, close enough that, at one time, she might have gotten all tingly. Yeah, well.

"Bar," she shouted back, since the only available tables appeared to require night vision goggles if you had half a hope of seeing the person you were with.

Somehow, Noah found them two stools. Jewel planted herself on one, then folded her hands tightly in front of her and ordered a Coke. Beside her, Noah chuckled as his phone buzzed. "Hate to break it to you," he said, checking it and texting a short message before pocketing it again, "but people don't come here for the ambiance, either. And I'll have whatever's on tap, Ramon," he said to the paunchy, steel-haired bartender. "And wouldja add a couple of burgers and fries to that?"

"Sure thing, Noah—"

"Trust me," Jewel shouted over an eruption of laughter behind them, "you don't want me getting drunk."

Noah's brow puckered as the bartender called out their orders to the cook in back. "No?"

She shook her head, smiling for Ramon when he set her Coke in front of her, then handed Noah his draft. "No. I sing, I cry, I throw up. Not necessarily in that order. What I do not do, is have fun. Nor does anybody who's with me."

"Then why are you here?" Noah took a swig of his beer. "Since it's pretty obvious you don't really want to be here with me."

Jewel sipped her Coke, wishing Noah would quit staring at her like he was trying to dissect her brain. She swung all the way around on her seat, surveying the jovial scene in front of her, forced though it may have been for many of the revelers. "Don't be silly, I can't think of a single person I'd rather be here with."

"Uh-huh."

Without moving her head, she cut her eyes to his. Like she couldn't see that smile behind the rim of his glass. She jerked her gaze away again, seriously reconsidering the not-getting-drunk thing. But only for a moment, since she knew that way lay idiocy.

"So why are *you* here?" she said. "With me, I mean?"

"Because shoving you out of my truck would've been awkward?"

She glanced over. "Any more awkward than going out with a girl your brother's—"

At Noah's arched brow, Jewel blushed and once more looked elsewhere.

Noah shifted to lean one elbow on the bar, his head propped in his hand. "You're right, there are some boundaries even I don't cross. Although, just to be clear—Silas hasn't said word one to me about what did or didn't go on between you. Not that it's not patently obvious something did—and if you ask me, still is—but Si's real good about keeping his private life private." His mouth pulled into a rueful grin. "As much as anybody can in this town. In this *family*."

Reaching across himself to grab his beer, Noah frowned at the glass for a moment before returning his gaze to hers. "So maybe all I'm doing is taking advantage of an opportunity—" he lifted the glass to his mouth, watching her as he swallowed "—to figure out for myself what was up with that ditzy act of yours."

Now she really wished she'd ordered something with more of a kick to it. "Ask Silas. We went all over that."

"So you *admit* it was an act?" When she nodded, Noah said, "Huh," then tilted the glass in her direction. "You almost had me fooled, I'll give you that. Si, too. Although that's not surprising, considering that what he knows about women you could put on the back of a matchbook."

"As opposed to you."

"That's right. Not that I pretend to understand why y'all do half the things you do, but at least I've gotten pretty good at pegging the good-time gals from the ones determined to get a ring on their finger."

"And I said—"

"I know what you said. And I think you had your reasons for not wanting to get tangled up. Obviously you still have 'em. But if I were to suggest we go back to my place for some good old-fashioned hanky-panky, my guess is you wouldn't exactly jump all over the idea. Or me."

Her eyes to his. "But you wouldn't do that."

Noah laughed. "In reality? No. Because A, that's not what you want and B, Silas would kill me. But in theory? If Silas wasn't my brother and you actually liked me...?"

"I do like you, Noah! It's just..."

"Go on. Say it. I dare you."

"You're a big meanie, you know that?"

"So I've been told," he said. Grinning. Jewel let out a shuddering sigh, then spun around to prop her elbows on the bar and her head in her hands.

"Dammit, it wasn't supposed to happen like this! Silas was supposed to be *safe,* he wasn't supposed to fall for me!"

"What on earth gave you the idea Silas was safe? Because you wanted him to be?"

She almost strangled on her own laugh. "I really am an idiot, huh?"

Their burgers arrived, the fries still sizzling in their little paper nests. Noah grabbed several and stuffed them into his mouth. "I assume that's a rhetorical question?" Jewel sorta growled at him. He laughed, then grabbed a ketchup bottle and shook it within an inch of its life. "You do know he hasn't even...dallied since Amy, right? Until you, that is," he said, drowning his fries, and Jewel thought, *Oh, hell-on-a-stick.*

"So much for his not saying anything."

"Even if you hadn't pretty much let it slip yourself a minute ago, the spring in Si's step the next morning kinda gave it away." When, groaning, Jewel let her head drop onto her arms, Noah said, "Which should've been your first clue right there, that things had changed. For him, anyway."

Head still down, she peeked up at him through crooked glasses. "Uh, yeah. Got that part."

The ketchup bottle thunked back onto the counter. "Then

did you also get the part where, unlike some of us here, Si doesn't get cozy simply because it's convenient?"

Slowly, Jewel lifted her head. "Got that, too. Not that he actually *said* he was, you know. Serious."

"Thought you just said he'd fallen for you?"

Despite her adamant refusal to do so before this, Jewel dredged up her memories of the look on Silas's face after they'd made love...in his kitchen the day she moved out. Now she wondered...was she remembering what she'd really seen? Or what...she'd wanted to see?

"I thought he had, but...maybe I imagined it. He said he'd never hurt me, and I don't doubt he meant it, but...oh, Lord, Noah—" she sighed "—all I want is for this to make *sense*—"

"And maybe," Silas said behind her, making Jewel spin around on the stool so fast she nearly fell off, "things might make more sense if you talked *to* me rather than about me."

Dear Lord, she could practically hear her blood pulse in her veins. Because what she saw in Silas's eyes—well, past the annoyed-as-all-hell thing—was honest and soul deep and *real*. And she wanted all of it—yes, even the annoyance, it made him human—so desperately it hurt.

Wanted it, yes. Trusted it?

No.

"Take me home, Noah," she said softly, sadly, sliding off the stool and heading toward the front as Silas's eyes burned a hole in her back, incinerating what last few scraps of dignity she had left.

Chapter Twelve

"Noah!" Although he'd already knocked, Silas thumped the heel of his hand against the door to his brother's apartment over the Meriweather's garage. "Your truck's parked out front so I know you're there!"

"Holy hell, Si," Noah said, yanking the door open. "Keep your shirt on."

He nodded at his brother's bare chest. "At least mine is."

"And I'm not usually dressed for company at—" rubbing his eyes, Noah made a face as he apparently tried to get a bead on his watch "—six-freaking-thirty in the morning." He grabbed a flannel shirt off the end of the sofa, shoving his arms into the sleeves but not buttoning it. "Where's the kids?"

"With Mom. They stayed over, she and Dad are taking 'em to church. Where's Jewel?"

"How the hell should I know? Although I'm gonna go out on a limb and say…her place?"

"Her car's not there."

"And did you see it here? No. So maybe she's delivering somebody's baby or something. Or here's another thought—you shook her up so bad she's fled to another state. Man, I need coffee…"

Silently fuming, Silas watched Noah lumber into the kitchenette a few measly feet from what passed for a living room, banging up the switch to the overhead light. The odd thing was, Noah could afford something better. And larger. He simply couldn't be bothered. "What do you mean, I shook *her* up?"

Noah hoisted the Maxwell House. "Caffeine first. Explanations later."

Like a dog with a bone, Silas followed, pulling two mugs out of the cupboard and automatically rinsing them out.

"Dude…" Noah yawned. "I'm a bachelor, not a cave man."

"Sorry. Habit. So…" Silas grabbed a dishtowel off the cupboard handle to dry the mugs. "You're saying nothing happened after you two left the bar?"

With a mirthless chuckle, Noah shoved the coffee basket into place and punched the on button. "Not that stupid, bro. Even if—" he yawned again "—she'd been even remotely interested. And we had that kind of relationship."

"You have 'that kind of relationship' with every female who crosses your path."

"And I'm gonna let that pass, but only 'cause I'm not awake enough to take offense." Ruffling his hair, Noah sank onto an open step stool, his bare feet hooked over the bottom step, to stare at the coffeepot, like he was willing it to brew faster. "But I swear—no, nothing happened. Other than her crying her eyes out for the next two hours."

"Good crying or bad crying?"

Noah pushed out a sigh. "All I asked," he said to the pot, "was five minutes. But no." Then soft brown eyes veered to Silas's. "And I know *you're* not that dumb, either. She's in love with you, butthead—"

"I know. She told me."

"She also tell you she's totally freaked about it?"

"In excruciating detail."

Noah gave him a did-I-miss-something? look. "You tell her you loved her?"

"Not in so many words, but—"

"Then you can thank me for filling in that particular blank."

"And why on *earth* would you do that?"

"Because you were too boneheaded to do it yourself? Because after two hours I was half ready to tell her *I* loved her if it would've stopped the tears? Because—here's a thought—it's the *truth?* But mostly because the two of you seem incapable of getting over yourselves and just getting on with it, already—as opposed to getting it on, which I gather already happened…oh, *thank* you, Lord."

At the coffeemaker's final, gasped gurgle Noah was on his feet, dumping the brew into his mug and indicating to Silas he was on his own. Three gulps later, Noah shut his eyes, exhaled, then gave his head a shake before looking at Silas again. "I don't think I've ever seen anybody more afraid to trust what she wants than that gal. All that crap she went through as a kid seriously messed with her head."

With a sigh of his own, Silas dropped onto the lone kitchen chair, a piece Eli had built as a sample for a client who then changed his mind. "Precisely why she needs the space to get that head screwed on straight."

"Okay, I was wrong. You are that dumb."

Silas cut his eyes to his brother. "Excuse me?"

Setting his mug on the table, Noah curled forward to lean his palms against the edge. "Okay, allow me to break this down for you. For all they made us nuts, the one constant in our lives growing up was that our parents loved us. Would always love us, no matter what we did, or how much we made *them* nuts. They weren't gonna go off and canoodle with somebody else, or play favorites—"

"Don't be too sure about that," Silas said, half smiling, and Noah leaned farther forward to take a wide swing at his head.

"My point is—except for that batty mother of hers, Jewel's never known what family is. Everybody she's ever loved has either run off, or been taken from her—"

"And it's left scars. Noah, you're not telling me anything I don't already know."

"I might if you'd shut your trap and let me finish. She doesn't trust love because nobody's ever shown her what that really means. From what I can tell, her mother's love comes with enough strings attached to put a spider to shame. Everybody's always expected her to be and do everything for them, but it's never gone the other way. When has anybody ever put their butt on the line for her? Dude. Being left *alone* is the last thing she needs."

Holy crap. Either the caffeine kicked in, or Silas was in revelation-readiness mode, but damn, that was a lot of light in his brain.

"Meaning, she's taking my backing off to mean...I don't care."

Noah sat back, his hands braced on his thighs. "Oh, believe me, she knows you care. But that's what scares her, because people have 'cared' before and left. Or changed their minds. Or pretended to care in order to get something from her. So I'm not talking about caring—I'm talking about 'you mean everything in the world to me' kind of love. The kind of love that's far more about giving than getting."

Silas looked at his brother like he'd turned into a pod person. "This, from the person who breaks out into hives at the mere suggestion of finding that special someone."

"My needs are not your needs, bro." He shrugged. "Doesn't mean I don't understand how it's supposed to work."

Silas pushed out a dry chuckle, then sat forward, letting Noah's earlier words sink in. "I really thought I was doing the right thing, letting her come to me. But until she felt safe enough to do that..." He stood, carting his empty mug to the maker for more coffee. "How could she?"

His second cup poured, Silas stood with one hand braced on the counter, frowning into the brew. "Even so, something tells me I could promise her 'til the cows come home I'd never abandon her and she still wouldn't believe me. Words are cheap."

"Damn cheap," his brother agreed, joining him at the coffee maker. "So you've gotta come up with, what is that called?" He lifted his refilled mug to him. "The Grand Gesture?"

"Like...hiring a plane to skywrite 'I love you' so the entire town can see it?"

"*God,* no," Noah said, and Silas smirked. "Oh. Sarcasm?"

"You might say."

His brother sank into what passed for deep thought, for him. "So what we need, is something that would make you look like a hero."

"What *we* need?"

"In a manner of speaking."

Silas snorted. "Get real. What could I possibly do..."

The thought slammed into him so hard he nearly spilled his coffee.

"What—?"

Silas held up one hand to his brother, thinking. Not that he had any clue how he could possibly accomplish it, but if it worked…

Oh, man.

Oh, *hell*.

The idea—it was beyond insane. The craziest, most out-of-control thing he'd ever even thought of, let alone actually tried.

Which meant he had to do it now, immediately, before the left side of his brain got wind of what the right side was thinking.

His heart punching his ribs, Silas finally met his brother's gaze. "Road trip?" he said, and Noah grinned.

"Jewel! Jewel!"

Whipping around so fast she nearly clipped another shopper with her basket, Jewel barely had time to catch her breath before both Tad and Ollie slammed into her legs, hugging her and splintering her heart into about a thousand pieces. Oh, heck, she thought, sliding to her knees to hug the boys back, laughing and dodging Tad's woodpecker-like kisses as she peppered both little faces with her own.

Yeah, this would be the hard part.

"What are you doing here?" she asked, the same moment she heard Gene Garrett's frantic "Boys? Where'd you go?" from over in the next aisle.

"It's okay, Gene, I've got 'em," she yelled back, because this was Wal-Mart and nobody would bat an eye, adding "Aisle Three!" for clarification. A second later Silas's father appeared around the endcap, huffing in exasperation as he trundled up the aisle toward his grandsons.

"What's the big idea, runnin' off like that?" he said in the manner of someone who clearly spoiled his grandchildren rotten, and a lump rose at the base of Jewel's throat which she quickly swallowed.

His arms still looped around Jewel's neck, Ollie said, "But it's Jewel, Papa!"

"An' we haven't seen her in forever!" Tad said, nodding vigorously. Then he turned to her, his mouth all turned down. "I miss you."

"Yeah," Ollie said. "Me, too. It's bor-*ing* without you."

"Yeah. Bor-*ing*."

"Aw," she somehow got out, "I miss you guys, too."

"Then how come you don't come see us?"

"Yeah. How come?"

"And you all talk too much, you know that?" Gene said, then pointed to the bakery a few feet away. "Why don't you go check out the donuts, decide what looks good. I'll join you in a minute."

The boys took off like a shot, leaving Jewel alone with Silas's father. Tee-rific. "Well. How's everything going?" she said brightly. "Donna healing up okay?"

"She's doing good," Gene said, gripping the freezer case handle and effectively preventing anyone from reaching the frozen fish. His gaze lifted to keep an eye on the boys. "And you?"

"I'm…doing well. Getting ready to move."

"Oh, yeah…that was quite a surprise, Eli selling his house that fast. Tess is one cracker-jack Realtor, for sure. He feels real bad about inconveniencing you, though. Look, if you don't find a place after the Blacks return, you can always stay with us now that Donna's sister's gone back home—"

"No, no…I mean, I appreciate the offer, really. But… that would be really awkward."

Gene gave her a funny look, until a mother with three kids in her cart shoved him aside to get to the fish sticks. "Yeah, I guess you have a point at that."

"How is Silas?" she finally asked, partly because it would be weird not to and partly because she really wanted to know.

"I suppose he's okay, although he's been out of town for a couple of days, so I don't actually know."

Jewel frowned. "Out of town?"

"Yeah." Another funny look. "With Noah. Personal business. Expect 'em back tonight sometime, in fact—"

"Papa!" Ollie hollered over, waving both arms. "We decided!"

"Okay, boys, I'll be right there. Well, Jewel," he said, angling his cart toward the bakery, "it was real nice seeing you. You take care, okay? And if there's anything you need, anything at all, you just let me or Donna know. I mean that."

"I know you do," Jewel said mostly to herself, watching him amble toward a pair of little boys she loved with all her heart. And with that, she decided it was now official:

She was flat-out miserable.

A misery that had relentlessly bloomed over the past couple of days, she irritably mused on the drive back to Eli's house, like the sniffles exploding into the Cold From Hell: knowing you'd eventually no longer want to chop off your own head was no consolation now.

And for the hundredth time she reminded herself her misery was all her own doing. Well, except for the communication cutoff from her stepbrother, that wasn't her fault. But walking away from probably the most wonderful man on the entire freaking planet because she was basically a big, fat wuss, only now she had no idea how to fix what she broke without looking like a big, fat idiot?

Yeah. If life was a comic strip, there'd be a big, fat red arrow pointing at her head right now.

"Brother," she muttered, walking into Eli's house and grimacing at the tower of taped boxes stacked in one corner. "When you screw up, you don't mess around, do you?"

Then there was the sidebar issue of alienating her mother. True, Kathryn's rosy-hued outlook on life would more than likely send Jewel to an early grave, but your mama's still your mama, and Jewel knew Kathryn loved her, in her own bizarre way. Cutting the woman out of her life entirely served no real purpose, that one brief, shining, illusory moment of freedom aside. If Jewel wanted to be truly free, she had to stop blaming her mother for her own mistakes, her own growing pains.

Not to mention cowering behind her dysfunctional childhood like that would somehow keep her from getting hurt, when actually all it did was keep her from *living*.

Loving.

Digging her new, you-can't-find-me-now cell phone out of her pocket, she bounced it against her mouth for a moment or two before punching in her mother's number. Because, you know, what earthly right did Jewel have to judge the woman for at least having the cojones to keep *trying* to find love? Funny, how she'd always thought of her mother as weak, when it turned out Kathryn was a helluva lot braver than her wimpy daughter.

Irony, she thought that was called.

"It's me, Mama," she said when Kathryn answered.

Several moments slipped by. Then: "You call to yell at me again?"

"No. I called to apologize for acting like…like a brat. I'm…I've been having kind of a rough time lately, and… and I took things out on you I shouldn't have, when the thing is…" Tears bit at her eyes. "I need my mama."

Not surprisingly, there was a real long pause. Then she heard her mother sniff. "Oh, baby...I don't think you've ever said that to me before. But then I don't suppose I've ever given you much reason to, have I? No, you don't have to say anything, I already know the answer."

Jewel picked at a loose thread on her knee. Man, this was hard. "You did your best."

That got a snort. "Like hell. I do not know where my head's been all these years, but for sure not where it was supposed to be."

Jewel held out her phone, staring at it a second before putting it back to her ear. Mama was still talking. "...after you gave me what-for in the restaurant the other day, I called Monty and cried bitterly about how you'd hurt me."

"I'm so sorry—"

"No, hear me out. When I'd finally finished blubbering, he got real quiet for a while. Then he started asking some pointed questions—he's got three grown kids of his own, so he's got more of a handle on being a parent than I do, I guess—and long story short, he made me look at things from a different perspective. He pointed out the tighter I held on to you, the more likely you were to slip through my fingers entirely."

"Really?"

"Yeah."

Jewel hesitated, then said, "You sound...different."

"I *feel* different. Like Sleeping Beauty," she laughed, "whose prince took his damn time getting here. But I'm thinking it was worth the wait."

"Wow. Monty..." Rolling her eyes, Jewel pushed out, "He sounds like a keeper."

Mama laughed softly. "That's what I'm hoping. Oh, baby, you have *nothing* to apologize for, believe me. It was me who messed up, not you." She paused. "But I'm curious—what was all that the other day about Keith and Aaron?"

"So you don't know?"

"Honey, I haven't exchanged word one with that man since I sent him packing. So, no—"

"Wait—you sent *him* packing?"

"You talk first. Then I'll fill in the blanks." Sure enough, after Jewel related the whole sad story, her mother sighed. "I knew how hard it was on you after Keith and I broke up, especially seeing how much you loved his little boy. I also know you blamed me for letting another daddy slip away. But when I found out Keith was cheating on me on all those *business* trips…that didn't exactly sit well. So I kicked him out on his ass."

"Oh, Mama…" Jewel didn't know whether to laugh or cry. "I had no idea."

"That was the plan." She huffed a humorless laugh. "At the time I was almost more mad at myself than I was at Keith, for being a damned fool. Bad enough I already felt like you were the adult and I was the child, even if I had no idea how to fix that. So my pride wouldn't let me admit I'd made another mistake. However, if you noticed I didn't exactly go off and get married again right away."

"But…all those boyfriends…?"

"Wanting to stay single is not the same thing as wanting to be *alone*. Even so, I wasn't *about* to get hitched again until I was sure I'd made the right choice."

"And you're sure about Monty?"

"Yes," Mama said, with more conviction than Jewel had ever heard before. "And I think if you'd meet him, you'd understand."

"Actually…I'd like that."

She heard her mother's voice hitch. "You mean it?"

"Of course I mean it. Whenever you want."

Mama hesitated, then said, "I know I'm repeating my-self, but please don't feel bad about what you said last week. I had it coming. I've had it coming for a long time. I know…I know I haven't exactly been there for you the way a mama should, but…I'd like to try now. If it's not too late, I mean."

Jewel scrubbed a tear off her cheek. "I'd like that, too. Could you…could you come up sometime? Like, soon?"

She heard her mother talking to somebody, then come back on the line. "How's this evening sound?"

"This evening sounds great…" At the sound of a truck pulling up outside, she struggled to her feet, massaging her numb butt as she walked to the window. Seeing Noah's pickup parked outside, she said, "Gotta go, looks like I've got company. See you soon."

"Love you, baby."

"I love you, too," she said, really, truly meaning it as she watched Noah unfold himself from behind the steering wheel. Then Silas popped out of the other side and her heart started thumping like mad in her chest. But not from fear, from excitement. Anticipation. The thrill of being *ready*.

Yeah, bring it, she thought, only to get another jolt when a moment later her stepbrother crawled out of the extended cab's back, all long limbs and big grin, and for a moment Jewel thought she might faint dead on the spot.

Trembling, she opened the door, vaguely aware of Silas grabbing Noah's arm as Aaron loped up the walk, break-ing into a full-out run before sprinting up the steps to grab Jewel around the waist.

"What…? How…?" Her head spinning, she wriggled out of his grasp, looking up into that goofy, adorable face that hadn't changed all that much since he was a toddler, truth be told.

"I'm here for good!"

"*What?*"

"You heard me! I'm gonna stay with Silas's and Noah's folks until…" His gaze swung to the two brothers, still back by the truck, and Jewel's gaze snagged in Silas's, which ramped up her heart rate quite nicely, thank you. "At least," Aaron said, his eyes on hers again, "until we figure out the next step."

"I don't understand," Jewel said over the dizziness.

"Does it matter?"

"Uh, yeah? Since I don't want the feds coming after me for kidnapping. Or something."

Aaron's brow furrowed. "I thought you'd be happy to see me."

"Oh, sweetie…" Her eyes watering, she threw her arms around him—as best she could being a foot shorter and all—and gave him another hug. "Of course I'm happy, that goes without saying!" She let go. "But your dad—"

"It was all Silas's idea," Noah shouted over, adding, after dodging Silas's attempted smack on his arm, "it's not like she's never gonna find out, you know."

Honestly. "Find out what?"

"Dude," Aaron said, "Silas was awesome. He shows up at my house, right? Then tells my Dad he's not leaving until Dad said it was okay for you and me to talk to each other again, and that if he tried to pull any of that 'inappropriate relationship' crap with you, he shouldn't be surprised if the IRS decided to get in touch with him."

Jewel's eyes bugged out. "You're kidding?"

"Nope. Then, while all this was going down? Witch Woman comes in, and her and Dad get into this humongous fight and the upshot was…" He shrugged. "He said if I wanted to go, he wouldn't stop me. So Silas made him sign this paper saying he couldn't change his mind…and here I am!"

Jewel met Silas's steady, hopeful gaze and wondered how she'd doubted for a single *second* that he loved her. "He…did all that?"

"Man, he was like one of those action flick dudes, storming the place to rescue me. Except without the storming. Or any explosions or stuff."

"Aaron?" Noah called. "What do you say we get you over to Mom and Dad's, let these two hash out a thing or two?" After another hug, the kid strode back to the truck, and Noah said, "And Jewel, you're expected for dinner, Mom said no excuses allowed."

"Oh!" Jewel said, crashing back to earth with a nice, hard bounce. "I can't, my mother's on her way. With her new fiancé."

"So bring 'em along," Noah said as Aaron climbed back into the truck. "The more, the crazier."

That would certainly be true, she thought as the truck disappeared in a burst of dust and dead leaves, leaving, when it all cleared, Silas standing in Eli's yard and Jewel with about five gazillion questions.

And one life-altering confession to make.

Silas's heart was thundering so hard Jewel could probably hear it from where she was. Which, at the moment, was much too far away.

And although he had no doubt she'd grill him as to the hows and whys that led to her brother's return, it was quite possible she'd never close that gap. And yet…the joy on her face when she hugged her brother had warmed Silas in a way few things ever had. Even if she couldn't, or wouldn't change her mind about them, he at least had the satisfaction of knowing he'd done everything he could to make someone else happy.

Anything else was buttercream icing on the cake.

"I don't suppose it occurred to you what an insane idea it was, going up there like that?" she said, obviously shivering, her voice floating to him on the soft breeze. Removing his jacket, Silas closed the gap himself to drape the garment over her shoulders, holding on to the lapels. To her.

"Only every thirty seconds from the time I thought of it until, well…" He smiled down at her. "Until I saw you two together again and realized sometimes the most insane ideas are the best ones."

"But…" Her eyes searched his. "There was no guarantee Keith would've said yes. What if he hadn't had anything to hide?"

Boldly, Silas slipped his hands around Jewel's waist and her hands landed on his chest and he thought, *Yes*. "All I could think of, after we…stopped seeing each other, was how nobody's ever really done anything just for you. So I asked myself…what did you most want in the whole world?"

Her eyes glittered. "And you thought of Aaron?"

"Thought that might have a mite more impact than flowers and chocolates," he said, and she giggled, and he realized how much he'd missed that giggle. How much he wanted to hear those giggles for the rest of his life.

"But how did you find him?"

"From the subscription label on that gaming mag he left here. Then I strong-armed Noah into being my wingman. Since he's bigger than me."

She snorted. "Except Noah wouldn't hurt a fly. Either."

"Yeah, but Keith didn't know that. And seeing how much you were hurting…I had to do something, anything, to at least convince him to let Aaron communicate with you again. Not that I had any idea how I thought I was going to pull it off," he added on a dry laugh, then drew her close again, inhaling something fruity this time. Nice. "I hate bullies, Jewel. Especially ones who enjoy making people miserable simply because it gives them some perverse sense of accomplishment. I know you were wrecked when Keith and your mother split, but believe me…it was for the best."

She was quiet for a moment, then said, "Yeah. I know that now. But at the time…" She sighed, then shifted to frown up at him. "Still. How on earth did you figure out that Keith cheated on his taxes?"

"I didn't."

Her eyes sparkled with something that made hope swell in his chest. "You were *bluffing?*"

"More like, I took a calculated risk. That somebody who'd take character swipes like he did at you probably wasn't scrupulously honest about his taxes. Especially someone with his own business with plenty of opportunity to cook the books. Judging by how pale he turned…bingo. Bullies all have soft underbellies, honey. Just have to figure out where they are."

"Wow." Mischief sparkled in her eyes. "Sexy *and* smart. Impressive. But…you're not really going to sic the IRS on him, are you?"

"Not that it's not tempting…but no. I shook loose what I needed, no point in being greedy. Or vindictive. Although when I saw for myself how Keith treated his own child, it was real tempting to go for the jugular, believe me."

"How sad," Jewel said, cuddling closer again. Encouraged, Silas smiled.

"In any case, what I hadn't counted on was Keith's significant other—'other' being the operative word, here—jumping on the opportunity to rid herself of a pesky, sullen teenager she'd never wanted, anyway."

"She's really Witch Woman?"

"Let's just say she and Keith seem to be a perfect match."

Another chortle tickled his chest, followed by a sigh. "What hell that must've been for my brother."

"A hell that's in his past now. My parents were in on this, which you've probably already figured out. In fact, kid's got more people here who love him than he'll know what to do with. Noah's already itching to take him under his wing."

Still snuggled close, Jewel moaned. "God help us all." Then she leaned back to look up at him, gratitude shining in her eyes, before softly grazing her knuckles across his late-day beard stubble. "So what happens now?"

"You and my parents have joint temporary guardianship of Aaron until the courts can sort it all out for good. But nobody's going to take him away from you again. At least, not until some cutie comes along and knocks the wind out of him."

Laughing, she grasped his hand and held it to her cheek, and his heart soared a little higher. "You're right," she said quietly. "Nobody's ever done anything like that for me. Or for Aaron, either, I imagine. Ohmigosh…" She looked into his eyes. "I can't believe you took such a huge chance."

"That Keith would give in—?"

"On me," Jewel whispered, smiling. "On us."

Silas took a breath. "That's what you do when you love somebody."

"Maybe so," she said, her eyes shiny. "But…while I'll be forever grateful to for bringing Aaron back…that's not the way to win my heart."

"But that's not why I did it! No matter what Noah might tell you—"

"I know," she whispered, her eyes never leaving his. "Which is why…it's yours. My heart, I mean. Turns out it wasn't freedom I was looking for, after all. It was courage. And if, after everything I've put you through, you're *still* willing to take a chance on me…I'd be ten kinds of fool not to return the favor."

Hardly daring to believe his ears, Silas stood there like a primo dork, staring at the woman. "I love you, honey. Although I could kick myself for not saying it sooner—"

"Silas?"

"Yeah?"

"Shut up and kiss me."

So he did, until some yahoo drove by and honked his horn at them in some lame attempt at ruining the moment. Except that was followed by another kiss that was far sweeter, especially when Jewel said, "You don't have to do anything to prove your love, Si. I knew that long before you brought my brother home. And what's more, I trust it. I trust *you*. But most important…I trust myself. That I can do this. That my love isn't going to go 'poof,' either. Because I won't let it."

He thought he'd pop. "Wow."

"I know, right?" Giggling, she touched her forehead to his chest. "I'm perfectly capable of taking care of myself. But you know what?" Her eyes lifted again, clear and free and unconflicted. "Turns out I'd much rather have company while I'm at it."

Taking another huge chance—was this getting to be a habit or what?—Silas reached into his pocket and pulled out the modest diamond ring he'd picked up on a whim before they'd left Denver. When Jewel gasped, he quickly said, "This is only a token of how serious I am, if you're not ready I completely understand. Sure, my parents eloped after they'd only known each other a month, but everyone thought they were crazy—"

"Oh, no, you don't."

"Oh. Okay," he said, starting to slip the ring back into his pocket, only Jewel laughed and grabbed his arm.

"No, goof. I mean—you want to propose, you do it right. Down on one knee." She pointed to the floor in front of her. "Now."

"Damn, you're bossy—"

"And you might not want to miss your window of opportunity when I'm feeling all overcome with gratitude and such. Because you never know when such a moment might come around again. Might even have to wait, oh, ten minutes."

Chuckling, Silas eased himself down on one knee, wincing at the hard floorboard. "Jewel Jasper...will you marry me?"

"You betcha—"

"But there's one condition."

"Oh?"

"Yeah. Aaron has to live with us or the deal's off."

Grinning, Jewel threw her arms around him, throwing them both off balance and onto the porch floor where they laughed and kissed and kissed and laughed, not even noticing the sound of the car pulling up into the driveway until Jewel's mother called out, "Sugar, is there something you want to tell me?"

Blushing furiously, Jewel scrambled backward off Silas, who didn't look even remotely embarrassed as he hauled her to her feet...and hooked his arm protectively around her waist, and she thought, *So this is what it feels like to have someone get your back. I like it.*

Because for the first time in her life, she felt truly safe, free to love and be loved without fear of either being taken advantage of or abandoned.

Holy mackerel. What a rush.

Jewel slowly lifted her left hand, letting the ring catch the light, and her mother squealed and clasped her hands together, then started toward Jewel, her arms extended.

Not quite ready to leave the comforting circle of Silas's arm, Jewel took in Kathryn's slightly shorter hair and more subdued boot-length skirt and suede jacket—still gorgeous, still sexy, but in a manner far more befitting someone in her middle forties rather than a time-warped twentysomething.

But it was the genuine smile, the kind brown eyes, beaming from the gangly, weathered-faced man scooting to keep up with her—the sun flashing off the sizeable chunk of turquoise in his bolo tie—that really snagged her attention, especially when he turned those eyes and that smile on her still-squealing mother, and it was clear as day the man was completely head-over-heels.

Would it last? Who knew? But it occurred to Jewel that it wasn't like we're only given a certain number of chances to get something right, whether you were talking baking the perfect cheesecake—which Jewel had yet to conquer but she hadn't given up—mastering a piece of music…or finding the right person to keep you sane. And a little bit crazy, too.

Then she looked up and saw Silas looking at her exactly the same way Monty was at her mother, all that endless, bottomless, limitless love, and a great calm came over her, and she realized there was nothing saying it had to take umpteen tries to get it right, either.

She stood on tiptoe to kiss her future *husband*—ohmigosh!—once more, then ran down the steps to hug her mother, her heart about to explode with happiness and the heady confidence that came with knowing that for the first time in her life everything was adding up exactly as it should.

And that the total promised to be infinitely more than the sum of its parts.

* * * * *

COMING NEXT MONTH

Available October 26, 2010

SPECIAL EDITION

#2077 EXPECTING THE BOSS'S BABY
Christine Rimmer
Bravo Family Ties

#2078 ONCE UPON A PROPOSAL
Allison Leigh
The Hunt for Cinderella

#2079 THUNDER CANYON HOMECOMING
Brenda Harlen
Montana Mavericks: Thunder Canyon Cowboys

#2080 UNDER THE MISTLETOE WITH JOHN DOE
Judy Duarte
Brighton Valley Medical Center

#2081 THE BILLIONAIRE'S HANDLER
Jennifer Greene

#2082 ACCIDENTAL HEIRESS
Nancy Robards Thompson

REQUEST YOUR FREE BOOKS!

2 FREE NOVELS PLUS 2 FREE GIFTS!

ᵀ Silhouette®

SPECIAL EDITION
Life, Love and Family!

YES! Please send me 2 FREE Silhouette® Special Edition® novels and my 2 FREE gifts (gifts are worth about $10). After receiving them, if I don't wish to receive any more books, I can return the shipping statement marked "cancel." If I don't cancel, I will receive 6 brand-new novels every month and be billed just $4.24 per book in the U.S. or $4.99 per book in Canada. That's a saving of 15% off the cover price! It's quite a bargain! Shipping and handling is just 50¢ per book.* I understand that accepting the 2 free books and gifts places me under no obligation to buy anything. I can always return a shipment and cancel at any time. Even if I never buy another book from Silhouette, the two free books and gifts are mine to keep forever.

235/335 SDN E5RG

Name	(PLEASE PRINT)

Address	Apt. #

City	State/Prov.	Zip/Postal Code

Signature (if under 18, a parent or guardian must sign)

Mail to the Silhouette Reader Service:
IN U.S.A.: P.O. Box 1867, Buffalo, NY 14240-1867
IN CANADA: P.O. Box 609, Fort Erie, Ontario L2A 5X3

Not valid for current subscribers to Silhouette Special Edition books.

Want to try two free books from another line?
Call 1-800-873-8635 or visit www.morefreebooks.com.

* Terms and prices subject to change without notice. Prices do not include applicable taxes. N.Y. residents add applicable sales tax. Canadian residents will be charged applicable provincial taxes and GST. Offer not valid in Quebec. This offer is limited to one order per household. All orders subject to approval. Credit or debit balances in a customer's account(s) may be offset by any other outstanding balance owed by or to the customer. Please allow 4 to 6 weeks for delivery. Offer available while quantities last.

Your Privacy: Silhouette is committed to protecting your privacy. Our Privacy Policy is available online at www.eHarlequin.com or upon request from the Reader Service. From time to time we make our lists of customers available to reputable third parties who may have a product or service of interest to you. If you would prefer we not share your name and address, please check here. ☐

Help us get it right—We strive for accurate, respectful and relevant communications. To clarify or modify your communication preferences, visit us at www.ReaderService.com/consumerschoice.

SSE10R

*See below for a sneak peek from
our inspirational line, Love Inspired® Suspense*

*Enjoy this heart-stopping excerpt from
RUNNING BLIND
by top author Shirlee McCoy,
available November 2010!*

**The mission trip to Mexico was supposed to be an
adventure. But the thrill turns sour when Jenna Dougherty
and her roommate Magdalena are kidnapped.**

"It's okay. I'm here to help." The voice was as deep as the
darkness, but Jenna Dougherty didn't believe the lie. She
could do nothing but lie still as hands slid down her arms,
felt the rope around her wrists.

"I'm going to use a knife to cut you free, Jenna. Hold
still."

The cold blade of a knife pressed close to her head before
her gag fell away.

"I—" she started, but her mouth was dry, and she could
do nothing but suck in air.

"Shhh. Whatever needs to be said can be said when
we're out of here." Nick spoke quietly, his hand gentle on
her cheek. There and gone as he sliced through the ropes on
her wrists and ankles.

He pulled her upright. "Come on. We may be on
borrowed time."

"I can't leave my friend," Jenna rasped out.

"There's no one here. Just us."

"She has to be here." Jenna took a step away.

"There's no one here. Let's go before that changes."

"It's dark. Maybe if we find a light…"

"What did you say?"

"We need to turn on the light. I can't leave until I know that—"

"What can you see, Jenna?"

"Nothing."

"No shadows? No light?"

"No."

"It's broad daylight. There's light spilling in from the window I climbed in through. You can't see it?"

She went cold at his words.

"I can't see anything."

"You've got a nasty bruise on your forehead. Maybe that has something to do with it." His fingers traced the tender flesh on her forehead.

"It doesn't matter *how* it happened. I'm blind!"

Can Nick help Jenna find her friend or will chasing this trail have Jenna running blindly again into danger?

Find out in RUNNING BLIND, available in November 2010 only from Love Inspired Suspense.